RICHARD T. COCHRAN

INTO THE
MYSTIC

THIS BOOK IS DEDICATED TO

DIXIE

Acknowledgments

Throughout my life, I have had the great fortune of being surrounded by angels. Some of them I have known all my life and some I have just met. Some I have never seen, but I hear them speak to me quite clearly. Others are very quiet, but I know they are there watching over me. The ones that make me smile the most are the ones that sing to me. I would most certainly not be the person I am without them. And for that I am thankful. Enjoy your angels...

RTC

CHAPTER

ONE

He had always found his rocking chair to be the best place for dissecting and examining his memories. The gentle back-and-forth motion took him back to earlier days, memories of happy times and the bittersweet remembrance of growth and innocence lost. Some were not so pleasant, even horrific, yet he still made room for them because they, too, cried out for recognition.

He reasoned that memories were the only true things he solely owned. Many of them were shared by the various friends and acquaintances he had come across through the days and nights that made up his experienced life, but all of them belonged to him.

He slowly turned and followed the path that had long ago been worn into the hardwood floor leading down the hallway of his house and saw that she had left on the small reading lamp in the corner of the library to his right.

The wondrous world of books had been opened to him as a child by his grandfather, who had assembled a fine library in his home brimming with fascinating tales of the outside world. Uncle Remus and wise kings shared dust-free shelves with mythical giants and Tom Sawyer. This refuge was filled with worn rugs from exotic lands, bowls of tasty nuts, a grand writing desk, and wooden sliding doors that closed out the noise of the city. There his grandfather had found sanctuary and comfort, often with a young boy on his knee to help him with his problems. More often than not, those problems had been solved before the child awoke from his nap, still in his grandfather's arms, oblivious to the fact that his presence had somehow been invaluable. The wisdom of his grandfather had perhaps been the most valuable gift of all—wisdom that had come from experience and had been freely given to the lucky few who shared his life.

As he stepped into the comfortable room, he caught sight of the worn bundle that had drawn him to the library in the first place. Picking it up, he returned quietly to the front porch and set it down outside.

The bundle, an old backpack, lay on the wooden porch and seemed to glow sporadically. His cat, Miler, sat next to it, and stared intently at the stored energy that pulsed from within the dusty and faded material.

The vexing backpack had appeared when his beloved wife Dixie had unearthed it from the deepest reaches of the attic as she gathered the requisite knick-knackery for the upcoming holidays. She had haltingly presented it to him for his inspection there in the library, not sure of the reaction it might elicit. She knew this would be of interest to him, for good or ill, but would leave it up to him as far as how to proceed. He cautiously stepped over the bundle of nervous fur that Miler had become and stood looking at the rocker.

His rocker had been made by his brother before the age of ten. Amazingly, the craftsmanship could rival any carpenter's, and it was made without the use of a single nail. He had carried this graceful chair with him from place to place, house to house, until he had found his sanctuary here and it had become a fixture out front on the high porch. The years of wear had left it in need of a good stain, and Lefty made a promise to himself that this would be the first task to accomplish after the holiday season. Dixie had other ideas about a timetable for the completion of this task, but for the moment his attention was on the backpack.

He cautiously picked up the bundle, breaking the trance that had taken control of Miler, and placed it in his lap as he slipped into the familiar chair. The small cat with the big belly found his spot to Lefty's left and assumed the familiar supine position that belied his moniker.

With his fingers, he tried to brush away as much of the accumulated dust as possible before opening the rusted zipper. With a gentle sigh of escaping air, the long-lost dreams and visions of an inexperienced young man that had occurred a lifetime ago floated out into the night.

The electricity of a time long past slowly began to return as he rummaged around inside, found the old bottle of Oaxacan tequila, and removed the dry and crusted cork. Tilting the empty bottle up to his lips, his entire body began to pulse and throb as he drank in the memory of youthful adventures. Out of habit, he blotted his dry lips with a faded bandana, replaced it in his back pocket, and wondered if he should continue. Having experienced this before, he had a good idea of what to expect.

He set the bottle on the worn wooden porch and reached for the journal that lay at the bottom of the pack, covered in a thin coating of tropical sand. As his fingers retrieved the yellowed testament, a wave of electricity ran up his arm and down through his loins, settling in his toes.

He slowly opened the journal and his eyes traced back over the words he thought he had written in a different time and a different place:

> I opened my eyes around Mile Marker 20. My third eye had been functional the entire trip and had seen the bayous of Louisiana; the cotton fields of Alabama, filled with the sweet harmony of old Negro spirituals; the coast of Mississippi, with the ancient shrimp boats that had been passed down from generation to generation; across the panhandle of Florida, with the final swoop straight down the state, crossing the Everglades and into the mouth of the Keys.

As our group passed Mile Marker 1, a great roar filled the air and swirled around the stale bus compartment. We were entering the Conch Republic...

Looking up from the journal, he watched the moon begin to rise behind some wandering clouds and trembled at the familiar sensations the journal had elicited. He realized that his eyes had become like large black marbles, and he once again saw with great clarity what had always been there before him. Turning to his left, he saw the festive, psychedelic yellow bus arrive at the corner and turn on its blinker. It would arrive at his home shortly and he would have his ticket punched for the last leg of the journey. He had signed up for the whole trip and it was his duty to finish. After all, he had come this far.

He again looked down at the journal as the brilliant full moon leaped out from behind the last of the clouds. A bolt of electricity coursed through his body, leaving him paralyzed. His hand was left on the page as if he were taking an oath and being sworn in to the membership of a secret brotherhood. He smiled as he watched the bus slowly pull up in front and park with a steamy whoosh of the brakes. The accordion door quietly opened and beckoned him. With the solace of a snoring cat to watch over him, he smiled once again and began to rock...

C H A P T E R

T W O

Austin, Texas
Sometime in the '70s

As the morning sun slowly crept across the
hardwood floor of his library, Lefty stirred
and silently rubbed his face. As his eyes adjusted
to the early light, he became aware that he had
again fallen asleep in his favorite reading chair
and not made it upstairs to their bed. He found
the tasseled bookmark that his grandfather had
given him on his eighth birthday and examined it
carefully. There, in his grandfather's worldly hand-
written script, was penned "Forget the destination. The journey is everything." He smiled as he
placed it in the book near the spine and closed
the volume that had acted as his blanket for the
last several hours. The sun slowly warmed the
room and he rose to begin the day.

Ceremony and ritual had always served Lefty well. It was a fixture in his life and he was uncomfortable when it was absent. He was a creature of habit, always thinking he knew what to do next, one foot in front of the other, rarely veering and relying on his "experience" to lead him in the right direction. Except for the aberrant misstep here and there, an unexpected journey or two, he enjoyed life by sticking to what he knew. He did, however, make room for "variances." Occasionally, he would crave the adventure and danger of something new, something he had never done before, and would jump into it with all of his being. But, again, this was not the norm.

As usual, the "children"—a pair of house cats named Bones and Pinkie—were sitting on the kitchen floor waiting for their breakfast. On the menu for today were the "Mariner's Special" and dried kibble. As the can of various fish parts was opened, the two cats began a slow drool that would have made Pavlov proud. As he mixed the two ingredients with warm water from the tap, the ceremony began. He crossed the antique floor and turned on the gas burner under the kettle. He reached into the bread box and retrieved two slices of rye bread, which he placed in the toaster. This happened every Sunday like clockwork—once again, ritual. He glanced over his shoulder only to see that the kids couldn't be bothered with this part of the rite and were only interested in what lay on the counter. Soon, the toast popped and the kettle began to whistle. He spread salted butter equally across the two pieces and, while waiting for it to melt, he prepared her tea. Today would be an orange spice blend of which Dixie was particularly fond. He carefully positioned the tea cozy over the pot and placed it on the tray, along with the toast and a sliced apple he had expertly cored beforehand. A crisp linen napkin finished the presentation and he ascended the stairs. He entered the darkened room and set the tray gently at the foot of the bed. He slowly opened the plantation shutters and let the filtered light ease gracefully into the space. Her face was hidden by pillows she had somehow accumulated during the night. He had never known anyone to do this, with the exception of his mother. They were alike in many ways and he considered them two of his best friends. Knowing she would be slow to rise today because it was the weekend, he kissed her arm and went back downstairs.

By this time, the two felines had worked themselves into a fine froth though they had not budged from their spots. They did not even turn to watch him upon his return. He checked to see that the kibble had sufficiently softened and then held the bowls aloft as if to offer communion on this fine spring morning. This was the signal for the two to split and wait at their appointed stations on opposite sides of the room. Pinkie's food was always placed down first so that she might enjoy a few moments of uninterrupted dining.

Now that the troops had been fed, he poured himself a glass of fresh juice and set it on the pine dining table. He went down the hall, opened the tall wooden door, and stepped out into the slightly cool morning air. He made his way down the steps and walked out into the morning dew that clung to each blade of grass, leaving a trail of footprints. The paper never seemed to be in the same place twice, but today, being Sunday, he was sure it could not be too well hidden. After awhile, he found it tucked behind one of the majestic oak trees that bordered their lot. The street seemed in order, quiet and sleepy.

The two kitties had finished their meal when he returned and were just beginning the long process of giving themselves a bath. Lefty had always found bathing to be a lonely business and much preferred a quick, cold shower. His father had always insisted that it was good for one's constitution. Of course, he had also told him that the best way to treat a compound fracture was to "walk it off" and to "rub some dirt on it."

Reaching into his jeans, Lefty pulled out his favorite Gerber lockblade and cut the string that held the paper together. This foot of cord would later be added to the now basketball-sized sphere he had accumulated, but not before the two cats had had their fun. Tossing the cord on the floor, he spread the paper out before him and scanned the headlines of each section. It had evidently been a slow night in the newsroom, nothing urgent, so he refolded the daily and pushed it to the center of the long table. He decided to move on to the most pressing of his needs, so he rose and went to the library. He perused his valuable collection of albums and made his decision. Monetarily, this collection was not valuable, but these 33 rpm discs of vinyl had provided the soundtrack to his life and were, on some level, irreplaceable to him. His choices were perfect for a spring weekend morning, and after a quick wipe with a dust cloth, he worked the center of the two records onto the spindle and clicked the lever. The first platter to fall was a performance by Edith G. Gassion, "The Little Sparrow", and better known as Edith Piaf. This French chanteuse had always intrigued him, as did his second selection, Billie Holiday. They both had died way before their time, but had lived life to its fullest.

Happy with the music choices he had made, he pulled out the key to his rolltop desk. He removed the spiral notebook that had been the center of his attention for the last several weeks and locked the desk. He strode back to the kitchen and found the cats fat and happy. They had sprawled across the floor after bathing, so he carefully stepped over them. Finishing his juice, he gazed out the large picture window that overlooked his garden and backyard and thought back on the events of the past few weeks.

Shortly after the first of the year, Lefty had received a cryptic letter from his longtime best friend, Pancho. He always reminded Lefty of a white rhino—broad, armored shoulders, built for speed, and very horny. The letter was written in his usual large block lettering, with no return address, and had arrived with postage due. Long ago, Pancho had started a tradition of underpaying his bills by one penny and this held true with his postage, too. He liked to think he was causing some social mischief, and to this day continued to do it. Lefty had carefully opened the envelope with his blade and found only two words—"Where to?" Lefty smiled and began to think about a destination for this year's excursion.

Over the years, the friends had invariably made a trip to a place they had never been before. These trips always happened in the spring and had become more daring each year. They started with places that were within driving distance, like New Orleans and the border towns of Mexico. The journey soon evolved into more faraway places like Amsterdam, Paris, and most recently, Kashmir, where they were exposed to the mystical East and the quest for spiritual truth. After returning from that trip, Lefty had researched the subject and found it to be of great interest to him. Pancho, too, was interested. Their studies had led them to a Native American spiritual guide or guru who had taught them much about Indian philosophy and the ritualistic practice of taking a sacrament to achieve a state of nirvana. This was not only right up their alley, it was practically banging on their back door.

Throughout the years, there have been innumerable stories told about thousands of experiences while under the influence of a relatively rare type of plant from the desert. None were exactly alike; all of them varied from trip to trip. The bending of time and space, along with vivid hallucinations, left each traveler with his or her own story to tell. The one constant was the belief that a communion with God and nature was somehow achieved. This journey of self-exploration was not without some danger. It might not be quite so pleasant to see oneself through unfiltered eyes. The optimal way to experience this would be under the guidance of a "road man," or someone who knew the way, during an actual ritual. Unfortunately, Westerners were seldom, if ever, allowed to participate in this shamanistic rite. Undeterred, Lefty and Pancho gleaned as much information as possible from their helpful guide and began to make plans.

As the weeks passed, Lefty had used the spiral as his bible and kept voluminous notes on what they might expect on their odyssey. Would they encounter a hellish vision of a world gone mad, or would they find themselves among the flowers that grew in the fields of heaven? Not knowing what to believe this journey would bring, he wanted—no, needed—to be fully prepared, and he tried to leave no stone unturned. He had spoken with a friend from the high country of Colorado named Annie Globes who could indeed provide them with the "sacrament" peyote, or, in the drug culture, buttons. The only problem was that Lefty would have to travel to the mountains to retrieve this commodity that was widely viewed as the coin of the realm for the spiritual world. That being decided, and the vernal equinox quickly approaching, the two friends felt they were ready.

Suddenly, Lefty's thoughts were interrupted by three crisp, official knocks on the front door. He could hardly expect a visitor bearing good news at 7:19 on a Sunday morning. The cats deserted the serenity of the warm kitchen in a singular blur, running low to the ground for maximum velocity. He thought for a long moment or two about not answering the door, but the annoying knocking resumed and Dixie's foot hit the floor in warning. Resignedly, he got up from the wooden chair and poked his head around the kitchen doorway, hoping that whatever menace was disturbing him had moved along. Two shadows were sharply illuminated against the smoked glass that filled the top half of the front entrance to his fortress of solitude while two small black figures sat motionless below, mimicking the inert statues outside on the porch. The shadows seemed to have no intention of retreating so Lefty tiptoed down the long hall. As he neared the door, he was able to make out that neither shadow appeared to be wearing a patrolman's cap. Thankful that the local constabulary was not there to handcuff his children and drag them away, he threw open the heavy door which slammed against the wall. He was met by two certified and, apparently, canonical young men in awkward apparel. Black shoes, socks, and pants were topped by a white short-sleeved rayon shirt and a black tie on both, and one of the characters sported very thick horn-rims. This seemed to be the uniform for the sale of new religion these days. Two older bicycles were lying on the lawn near the sidewalk. Curious as to why these young men might be reduced to riding bicycles to his house this early in the morning, Lefty opened his mouth to speak, but was interrupted by the bespectacled one, who politely asked, "Are those animals dangerous?" Lefty looked down at the two cats and grinned, saying, "I don't know. Let's find out. Attack!" Both of them stood slack-jawed and frozen with fear. After a moment of tension, the cats countered the two intruders' step backward with one step forward. When Bones tired of this exchange and began to yawn, the two, fearing an eminent attack by this fanged feline, dropped a dozen pamphlets in their haste to retreat to the relative safety of another block. Lefty picked up the impassioned literature and quietly closed the door, thinking that next time he would answer the door in only the suit God had given him so many years ago. Breezing through the information in the pamphlets, he heard movement from the top of the stairwell.

"Honey, what's going on down there? Was there some kind of accident? Did someone die? It is way too early on a Sunday morning for the neighborhood kids to be making a racket like that. If I catch those Jackson misfits 'ringing and running' again, somebody's going to pay."

"No, sugar, it wasn't them. That'll probably happen sometime tonight. But it appears that somebody did die, though. According to this literature, it seems Jesus died a few years back and it was all on our behalf," Lefty stated smugly. Dixie slammed her door shut, returning to the breakfast he had brought her.

CHAPTER THREE

Lefty had always found Austin energizing in the spring. The funk of a wet winter was usually washed away before mid-March, when the music seemed crisper, the girls a bit prettier, and life a little peppier. There always seemed to be one day that triggered this change of seasons and today was it. First things first. He needed to collect the necessities for the upcoming adventure; a trip of this magnitude required lots of preparation, supplies, and forethought. He made a meticulous shopping list and set out into the bright morning sun.

The Hyde Park area of town was a sight to behold this early in the morning. His neighbor, Townes, was shooting at some whiskey bottles with a pellet gun and saluted Lefty as he passed. Townes, when sober, was regarded as the sheriff of the neighborhood, and often patrolled the streets after his target practice with a guitar slung across his back and a goofy smile on his face. Lefty returned the salute as he turned the corner, made his way to Eloy's and ran up the steps. He took his usual spot near the rear and waited for the routine to begin.

Tortilla Flats was the name on the door, but anyone who had met the proprietor knew this was Eloy's. Eloy was a Dartmouth-schooled Cuban refugee with a master's in literature. He was working on his doctorate when he discovered his skills in the kitchen. He was also working on his Carmen Miranda impersonation, but that was another story for another day. Tacos were his passion, and he was nothing if not passionate. He didn't look up when Lefty arrived; his nose remained planted in a collection of Hemingway novellas from which he wouldn't be distracted. Besides, the routine hadn't even started.

Like many things Lefty did, routine had turned to ritual, and ritual became a cornerstone of his day. The routine began with the arrival of a lovely, slim Mexican girl carrying a *molcajete*— a rough mortar and pestle from Mexico—and various bowls of spices. Her name was Caroline and her slimness made her an anomaly at Elroy's. Her long lashes were the most prominent of her many interesting features. They seemed to almost undulate when there was even the slightest breeze. Her skin was creamy and fresh, like the aroma that filled the air inside the *taqueria.* In days gone by, when she and Lefty had first shared a smoke outside one her classes, he had learned she had been a hellion and a bit of a tramp. She had a way with words and often described herself as an "ex-trollop." But that was a long time ago. She now had four children of various ages, although all were less than thirteen. Being a single mom, the children often accompanied her to work when her shift began at five a.m. From there, they would catch various buses to school, one by one, as the sun grew higher. Today, being the weekend, they were at home doing their assigned chores.

Eloy's personified the spirit of communal life in Austin at that time. People would just drop by between classes to sit around and shoot the breeze or to help out in some way. Lefty felt at home here and often started his day at a table near the back.

He positioned the bowls in front of him and began to grind. One by one, the bowls of seeds were ground, always saving the cumin for last. It was the most fragrant and his favorite. It was evidently also Eloy's favorite because he used it in almost every dish. As he brushed the last of the finely ground spice from the *molcajete* and into the bowl, as if on cue, Eloy looked up and silently raised one finger, then two. This was his way of asking how much nourishment was needed today, a single or a double. Lefty raised his hand with the familiar forefinger-pinkie two fingers that unified Austin football fans each fall. Indeed, two fingers were needed today for the energy to finish his shopping. Eloy jumped into action.

Lefty sat back and admired the familiar décor. Besides two small shelves that held cheap Mexican pottery, the walls were covered with all manner of posters. The placards were of anything that amused Eloy. Velvet bullfighters, Che Guevara, and popular rock musicians were the most prevalent. Leaflets featuring local bands littered the wooden pillars that supported the structure. The bathroom walls were a collection of graffiti, both humorous and scatological, that vaguely resembled Eloy's penmanship.

Lefty's two tacos arrived with a smile and extra portions of salsa verde. The recipe for this salsa was closely guarded and was rumored to have come from the hacienda Casa de Sosa in Cuernavaca. This grand estate was said to have many of the finest *cocineras,* or chefs, in Northern Mexico employed there.

A two-fingered order consisted of one *lengua* taco and one egg and bacon taco. He quickly devoured the "breakfast" part of his meal and wiped his hands. Lefty was especially fond of the *lengua.* He also knew he would never have even tasted it the first time if he had known it was tongue. He had only tried it after a four-finger night of tequila, when he had thought it was rare roast beef. The tacos were accompanied by tomatoes, onion, cilantro, and avocado. He relished the flavors, ate every bite, and carefully cleaned his lips of any remnants.

He casually pulled the shopping list out of his pocket and began to review it. Most of the items were easy to procure. In fact, five of the eight could be obtained within a seven-mile radius. Even better, two of them were less than a block away. He carefully folded the list and put it in his shirt pocket. He found two crumpled one-dollar bills in his jeans' pocket and put them on the table. Although not needed, they were appreciated by his friend.

"I hear you and Pancho are going on your annual adventure soon," Caroline said as Lefty approached the doorway. "I know it would be like preaching to the choir to ask, but have you thought this thing through? I mean, have you done your homework? I just don't want to have to read about it in the papers again like last time. Hell, I didn't even know where Zanzibar was until I heard that you two had been, shall we say, 'detained'? Impersonating a diplomat, I believe. Sometimes you need to throw on the brakes when Pancho gets that look in his eye."

Lefty stood there looking at the ground and moved some dirt around with his boot. He finally looked up, shrugged his shoulders, and said, "What are you gonna do? You know, I get him in as much trouble as he does me. I'm just better at making a clean escape." The inside joke made them both smile as he scooted out into the light.

Cuthbert's Cutlery would be the first and closest stop. A small paring knife, preferably a Henckels, and a foot-long Bowie knife were needed. The small knife's use was clear. The Bowie was for...well, the unknown. New lands loomed and the danger that was inherent with a major journey could not be underestimated. A twelve-inch blade of glimmering steel, even when used as a bluff, could stop an unpleasant argument rather quickly. He narrowed down the Bowie to two choices—"The Widow Maker" and "The Eye-Opener." He chose the former purely on style points and paid the bill. Two more stops were needed to complete his quest for the short-range items. The others would be more difficult.

Chapter
Four

Thanks to a found student ID card, Lefty was able to traverse the city fairly easily using the university's bus system—ancient conveyances that were free to students and the occasional homeless person. The university's maintenance department evidently had no knowledge of shock absorbers or brakes because not one of the buses seemed to be equipped with them. They bumped and rolled on the smoothest of streets and needed several car lengths to come to a complete stop. Despite this, Lefty appreciated a free ticket when he had one, and after climbing aboard he slipped into a seat near the rear and closed his eyes.

At the next stop, the door crashed opened and he noticed two men wearing turbans get on. They spoke in hushed tones, a distinctly foreign language, possibly Farsi, and became more agitated as they approached their seats. They seemed to be arguing about something important. Having never been to Persia, or anywhere else in the Middle East for that matter, Lefty didn't have a clue as to what they were saying and figured it was just as well, as long as they didn't throw off their turbans and begin to pummel each other, much less him. Three more stops and he would be getting off, anyway. His mind drifted as he envisioned a melee between the two men where lances were thrust and blood spilled. This was somewhat entertaining, but he soon lost interest. He put his cheek against the window and watched the passing sights.

As the bus moved along down Guadalupe Street, otherwise known as the Drag, a vagrant boarded and limped down the aisle, collapsing onto a seat. He wore some type of dirty poultice on his right leg that appeared to ooze a particularly viscous liquid from around the edges. The last passenger to board at this stop was a prim, if not proper, librarian looking for some relief from the morning sun. This librarian caused movement in Lefty's southern hemisphere, but he knew this was no time for philandering. He had always secretly believed all librarians, his junior high one in particular, to be closet nymphomaniacs. He thought of her glasses being thrown into the air as passion caused her to rip off her dress, revealing a bustier and nylons. Her brown hair would be allowed to escape from the confines of a barrette and fall down across her shoulders into the cleft of her backside. There, deep in the deserted stacks, she would take his virginity and ravish him. He would explode inside of her and...

Lefty shook his head violently, rousing himself awake and back to the matters at hand. He had always been interested in the notion of love and danger, and here he had found it all on the same bus. Knowing his stop was next, he begrudgingly rose and exited the vehicle.

The first stop was at a quaint convenience store that fronted for a bootleg house. Due to the antiquated blue laws forbidding the sale of liquor in Texas on Sundays, those needing spirits on that day had to use an operation such as this. This one was run by a lively Texan—appropriately nicknamed "Tex"—who was partial to Lefty. All it took was a call the day before and the goods were available by the next morning. The only negative was that Tex would want to chat with him for the better part of an hour and his incessant yammering drove Lefty crazy.

The retail sale of liquor on the Sabbath was indeed illegal, and this gave Lefty pause. These supplies were needed for the adventure, but Lefty would hate to grab a room at the "Iron Hotel" should some wayward constable darken the doorway and spoil the party before it had even started. This was taking a chance, but Lefty knew that it would only be the first of many chances to be taken over the next several days. He brushed aside his worries and strode into the store confidently.

After Lefty asked if his order was ready, Tex ambled through a gingham curtain that separated the two sections. He returned with the two bottles Lefty had requested, a liter of fine mescal and a dusty bottle of 100% pure blue agave Anejo. These two items would most likely be needed to take the edge off their trip once they began their return from the outer regions of inner space. The bottles had been wrapped in newspaper with a cardboard divider and placed in a brown paper bag. A loaf of day-old seven-grain bread was thrown on top to further the disguise. The transaction was completed, and luckily a tourist entered to ask for directions. Lefty used this opportunity to escape, waving and giving his cheerful grin as he bounded out the door, happy to have accomplished his mission without wasting his time nattering with Tex.

Whole Foods Market was a wonderful organic grocery that had originated in Austin. It had a marvelous selection of produce and meats, and hopefully the strong Cuban espresso and key limes that Lefty coveted. He was not usually a coffee drinker, normally drinking only decaffeinated herbal tea, but he knew that in the next few days he would need a buzz in his shoe to make sure that everything was completed on schedule. After finding some nice Café Pilon, he made his way down the fruit and vegetable aisle, where he noticed two foreign women examining some baking potatoes. Bending low to grab a paper produce bag, Lefty's head momentarily disappeared behind the turnip bin.

Marisol, the older of the two, said calmly, "Pilar, these potato, they remind me of the testeecals of me Poppi."

Pilar's eyes opened wide, and after making sure there was no one within earshot, she said quietly, "You mean they are thet beeg?"

Without skipping a beat, Marisol said, "No. They thet durty."

Lefty cracked his head on the wooden boxes so hard that he collapsed on the floor. The woman seemed so matter-of-fact in her response that he found the entire conversation patently absurd. After a moment of tension, the two ladies exploded with laughter, clapping each other on the back. After regaining his composure, Lefty grabbed several of the desired limes and hastily made his way to the checkout counter.

After paying, he headed back to the Drag, where he found the mix of eclectic bookstores, boutiques, head shops, and buskers, along with the various street people and an occasional feral dog that gave the Drag its character. Finding the stationery store he was looking for, he opened the door and stepped into the cool air. This was where he needed to purchase possibly the most important item on his list. The smell of new paper greeted him as he browsed the aisles looking for the diary. It would be used to chronicle his adventures with observations and perceptions captured during the journey. He found a leather-bound one that was small enough to easily carry in his jeans and paid the brown-eyed girl at the register. A short bus ride and he was on his home turf again, prepared for the adventure ahead as well as he felt he could be.

CHAPTER
FIVE

As he made his way back to the house, he once again noticed the dearth of squirrels in the neighborhood, mostly because the dogs on the ground and the cats in the trees had conspired to rid the area of the furry rodents. It was rare that these two species worked so well in tandem. Lefty didn't have much use for dogs. Cats were a different story, though. Like him, they were independent, clean, and mysterious. They came and went when they pleased. They were smart enough not to eat everything put in front of them and they didn't drool except at mealtime. They would often run from room to room at top speed without cause as if they were chasing phantoms, or stare at blank walls like the very meaning of life had once been scribbled there but now had become invisible to the human eye. Lefty often thought of himself in those terms, as a part of his character—not the cute and cuddly ball-of-fur and nonchalance part, but the inquisitive, playful, and adventuresome side associated with cats. After all, he had been known to chase a phantom every now and again.

Lefty and Dixie were lucky to have two of these unusual rascals. They were actually orphans that had adopted Dixie. They had appeared separately but soon had become brother and sister. Although both were black American shorthairs, they couldn't have been more different. Bones, the male, actually thought he was a dog. He would follow Lefty wherever he went, sometimes following him for blocks as he visited neighbors. If they were sitting on the front porch and a familiar dog walked by, Bones would leap off the porch and greet the animal warmly. This confused many a canine and often its owners. Bones had acquired his moniker from his repeated attempts to open doors by trying to ram them with his skull. He had been christened "Bonehead," which eventually was shortened to Bones. Lefty had wondered if the repetitious pounding of the cat's cranium had caused him permanent brain damage, thereby explaining his right political bent and why he had become, as Lefty had always said, a "ripe banana Republican."

Bones was peculiar for many reasons, but there were two things that particularly stood out. First, he was a talker. Lefty was never quite sure whether Bones actually spoke English, or if it was that he spoke cat. But he did know that he and Bones could communicate with each other better than a lot of people from the neighborhood. They would sit in the rocker on the high front porch and discuss a myriad of topics, sometimes until early in the morning. You would think that a cat wouldn't know crap from Crisco, but Bones was a different breed of cat, if you will. One night they might discuss biblical scripture and prophecy, and the next, early Miles Davis. Bones was knowledgeable in many areas, particularly those that involved the human mind and how it worked. Sometimes Lefty wondered who was the teacher and who was the student.

Second, Bones was a Jimi Hendrix freak. If Lefty was in the library and Bones returned from some nefarious adventure, he would plop down in front of the left speaker and stare at it. That was Lefty's cue to get up, move across the room, clean the needle of any stray balls of dust, flip through the lineup of LPs and select an appropriate disc. Bones's favorites were *Live at Monterey* and *Electric Ladyland*. Since he also fancied himself a watch cat, "All Along the Watchtower" had become a new request. After the first few verses, he would roll over on his back and, using all four paws, juggle a catnip-filled ball like a Kodiak bear in a Russian circus. After a while, he would tire, or if the catnip was fresh, he would pass out and begin to snore. Catnip was a funny aromatic herb originally from Europe that was purported to have medicinal qualities for humans and was often used to relieve gas. Once, Lefty tried it to see what would happen, but as usual it had the opposite effect on him, and he toot-toot-tooted around like a little motorboat for the remainder of the afternoon.

Pinkie, on the other hand, was a delicate little female who mostly stayed under the bed or in a closet for the majority of the day. Nighttime was her domain and she roamed freely under the cover of darkness. What was she was up to on her nocturnal jaunts? Hunting? Haunting? Exploring? No one was sure, although she had sometimes been spotted crossing the road under a streetlamp carrying something suspicious in her mouth. She rarely spoke, purred all day long, and loved to have her ears pulled. She might be under the bed hidden away from human eyes but her purr eventually gave her away. She had no use for the usual cat toys, not even the scratching post, and yet she still possessed needlelike claws. She would peek one eye around a corner and think she was invisible. It had always amused Lefty and Dixie to look down the long hall to the library and see one ear and one eye staring at them as they worked a crossword or read the paper in the kitchen. The eye never blinked, and seemed to be frozen until movement was made in her direction, at which time she would slowly retreat backward until even her whiskers were gone.

After Lefty put away his purchases, he scoured the house looking for some signs of life. Finding none, he scrawled a note to Dixie that he would be next door at Cal's and put it where everyone would see it—above the cats' water bowls in the kitchen. There, he was amazed to find a telegram for him. Ms. Annie from the high country had wired to say there had been a change of plans and she would be arriving in a day or two, bringing with her the "party favors," the final component needed for their journey. He would not have to travel to the high country after all!

Just the week before, he had gone to the old freight yards on the edge of town to see if it was still possible to make your way across the country in the relative comfort of a straw-filled boxcar brimming with interesting characters with names like Whispering-Lies McGruder, Boxcar Greg, and Sir Francis Drank. Life on the rails had always greatly intrigued him, and in his youth he would spend countless hours watching the trains clickety-clack down the track leaving mashed pennies in their wake. Pancho had often ridden the rails under the pseudonym "Poo-Knickers" Willie, while Lefty had used "Can-o-Peas" Mel after an incident that had occurred around a campfire somewhere outside of Tulsa involving a large quantity of spodee-odee wine, a fork, and a can of peas. So, if possible, he wanted to make this adventure as truly authentic as it could be by hopping a northbound freight and watching the world pass by.

Unfortunately, the romance of riding the rails had long been gone. Ruthless gangs of felons had lately replaced the amiable tramps and hoboes that were once a staple of transcontinental travel. Yard detectives, or "bulls," were not as understanding as in yesteryear and fences now surrounded the tracks. As he was turning to leave, he thought he caught a waft of hobo stew floating in the air, which brought back many memories of the earlier days. Later that afternoon, he had called the train station to inquire about the possibilities of catching a fast train to the high country and was pleasantly surprised to find that it would be no problem. It would also be relatively cheap and infinitely more comfortable. Although he was ready and willing to go, Annie's visit to him would allow him more time to finish any last-minute details that would invariably arise before leaving on his adventure with Pancho.

With the burden of travel now removed, Lefty opened the back door and stepped out into the splendor of his yard. Dixie had a green thumb and it showed. She had flowers that were blooming and her garden was already planted. By summer, there would be tomatoes, cucumbers, carrots, peppers, green beans, and black-eyed peas, probably some lettuce if the rabbits behaved, and maybe even some sweet corn along the back fence. He stood admiring the results of her talents and was glad that the grass was not yet growing rapidly. Perhaps by the following week it might deserve a trim, but for now all was well. He looked up and over the fence between the adjoining houses, saw Cal's red flag flapping in the wind, and hurried over.

CHAPTER
SIX

Cal was the neighborhood alchemist and had
been a close friend of Pancho's for many
years. Lefty knew him through that connection
and they, too, had become quite fond of one
another, so much so that they became neighbors. Quite by accident, Cal had found a home
right next door to Lefty and Dixie that fitted his
needs, mainly a large work area/garage where
he piddled with various "projects." He had an
intense personality and walked in a crouch, with
his knees bent. He reminded Lefty of Groucho
Marx prowling a stage, except that he was much
more frenzied in his movements, always seemed
to be in a hurry, and didn't smoke cigars, choos-
ing instead to inhale the noxious-smelling clove
cigarettes of which he was so fond. He had a
vaguely Mediterranean look, roguish and sturdy,
with a Roman chin and nose. His canine teeth
looked as though they might have been sharpened

with a rat-tail file and he loved to flash them with a growl during normal conversation. He had eyes that could pierce your soul and he used them to his advantage to intoxicate young ladies out of their delicates. He was highly educated and loved to tinker on projects that piqued his interest. He invariably had several going at once, and had the ability to keep them all separate, like so many plates in a juggler's hands.

He had recently inherited a small four-seater plane, a T-41 Mescalero, which was in some dis-repair. It was similar to a Cessna 172 and had a flight range of almost eight hundred miles. He had received his pilot's license and was instrument-rated within a few years when he decided to refurbish the plane. He had done a splendid job, and Lefty enjoyed the afternoons they had spent soaring high above the Texas Hill Country.

Presently, Cal was tinkering on a new type of fuel for the plane, one that would almost double the flight range. With a fuel capacity of only about ninety-eight gallons, he was also working on rigging an extra tank on board to further extend the scope of travel.

There were certain projects that were not common knowledge on the block. This was one of them, and ever cautious, Cal had devised a flag system. A red flag flying was an invitation to come over, drink a Shiner, spit, and tell some lies. A black flag was a warning to stay away. It also meant that the gate would be padlocked, the front shades drawn, and a fierce English bulldog named Holy Shit that was ugly enough to make

Ray Charles flinch would be attached to the front porch on a twelve-foot chain. Lefty had learned to keep some kibble in his pocket just in case he needed to find Cal during a black-flag session. Being a confidante, Lefty had been in the laboratory many times, and was always amazed to see what his buddy was up to on any given day.

As Cal lifted the Navajo blanket that secreted the lab from the rest of the garage area, the oily smell of tools and rags filled their nostrils. As usual, they donned lab coats and protective eyewear, for Cal did not want an accident on his watch. A small workbench lined the back wall and a lamp that had long ago lost its shade shone light around the small space. Large boxes of files lined another wall, and opposite that were three card tables on which sat beakers and Bunsen burners of every size and description. Lefty had always wondered about the pitfalls of mixing different petrochemicals, but Cal had assured him there was no peril.

"Cal, I think you've probably heard by now that Pancho's coming in, it being spring and all, and there is this trip we're gonna be taking next weekend. We are going somewhere we aren't really familiar with, somewhere I believe you have gone before, and I was wondering if you might see your way to be our wingman on this one. It might be a little more than we signed up for, if you catch my drift. A gal friend of mine from Colorado is gonna shoot down with some peyote buttons for us and I'm sure there'll be enough to go around."

Cal slowly lowered his head to his chest and mumbled to himself, "Christ, just what I needed right about now...two would-be 'space cowboys' zooming around in another galaxy, then wanting me to steer them back home." His eyes roamed around the cluttered room for several minutes before he asked, "What in the hell are you two doing buying that shit from Colorado, anyway? You *know* those buttons grow out in the desert! At least, the good ones do. Nope, count me out. Not this time. More than once a month might be just too much. Remember that little Asian chick I've been crazy over for the last couple of weeks? Well, we tried something very much like that a few weeks ago and I'm still not sure what the hell happened. Didn't even know what the shit was when we took it. Still don't. Got more scrambled than Aunt Terri's eggs. Anyways, I'm hooking up with her next weekend and I need to be in fine form...or as close to it as I can be." Lefty had already processed the answer and began to wonder what the adventure might have been like with a veteran warrior along for the ride. Noticing his lack of attention, Cal asked, "What do you say about a game?"

Washers, or "redneck horseshoes," seemed to be a uniquely Texan game, or at least that was the way Lefty saw it. It was akin to horseshoes, in that you were throwing an object at a goal and trying to get as close to it as possible, except with washers you weren't slinging two pounds, eight ounces of iron at your competitors after several beers. You could easily purchase this game for a few dollars from a grocery market and a hardware store. Two cans of any soup you might enjoy with a grilled cheese sandwich on a cool fall day and a handful of Fender washers and you were good to go. You needed to dig a hole, place the empty soup can into that hole, and replace the dirt around the lid until it was flush with the surrounding soil level. Repeat on the other end of the court and you were ready for a fun afternoon.

"You know, Left, I got my game goin' real good here for a bit, and I was thinking that if you and I could toss a lot more washers over there,"—pointing to the other end of the court— "instead of tossing back so many dang Shiners over here, we might just be good 'nuff to make a run at Luckenbach and hang around a bit in the finals. I'm tired of those boys from Tyler keepin' all the hardware every year. I found that stretch of Astroturf out back of Greenway's Five and Dime. We can clean it up a little, invite the right kind a player—you know, the type that might think nothing about throwing a few hints our way—get our game right where it needs to be, and who knows? I know for sure that mantel of yours is just collecting dust! What do ya say? You in?"

After a moment, Lefty said, "Yeah, maybe." He was still focused on the trip and his mind was elsewhere, but it was his turn to toss.

Lefty had the choice of colors today since he was the guest. He chose the dark blue Cowboy washers, so Cal was left with the powder blue Oiler ones. Lefty had always been a fan of the Cowboys, and besides his father, his childhood heroes had been Bob Lilly, Mel Renfro, and Don Meredith. In fact, his first dog had been named Dandy as a tribute to the fun-loving Meredith.

As he had predicted, Cal was spot-on in his tossing and was winning, but Lefty didn't mind. He was in a good mood and quite comfortable. At four o'clock, it was decided that it was beer-thirty. Cal went to the garage and opened the antediluvian GE refrigerator, the door of which was layered in stickers, and produced two frost-covered Shiners. He pointed to a new sticker he had just acquired that read "Beer—Breakfast of Champions!" and grinned. After taking Holy Shit off the chain and coaxing him into the house, they moved to the front porch and took their seats on the large wooden swing Cal had just bought at a garage sale for a dollar. Two new slats, a coat of paint, and it was almost as good as new.

Cal was an expert at the garage sale game. He could find a jewel in the rough that others passed over, and even if it needed a little work, could revive the item and give it new life. He had found many of the components for his projects at these sales or in someone's trash. He would study the Thursday and Friday classifieds to find the sales and plan his route for the weekend, always starting early before the advertised time. Occasionally, he would hit those sale sites on Sunday evenings when the items not sold were just tossed on the parkway for Monday pickup, and he did his own little cleanup.

The sun began to tire from warming the day and slowly fell behind Mount Bonnell. Not having much to do for the next day or three, it was determined that it was a good night for singing—and maybe even a little dancing.

Dixie swung into the driveway on two wheels spraying gravel into the air. She spent her days as a volunteer at the county wildlife refuge, and tonight she was ready to let her hair down.

"Hey, boys! What are you talking about? Girls? My ears were burning!" Dixie yelled playfully.

Lefty rolled his eyes and sighed. So close to a clean getaway! He gave her the ooshka-ooshka look and she laughed. "Hon, it might be time for one of your mowing parties. These weeds are getting mighty brave and are sticking their heads up!"

Lefty looked at her over his shoulder, rolled his eyes again, and yelled back, "*That* can wait. *You* go get your boogie shoes on. I think I smell a party tonight. Get changed and bring over some supplies." Dixie waved and disappeared into the house. After an absurdly long forty-five minutes, she emerged looking almost exactly the same.

Dixie brought along some goodies for this shindig that did not disappoint—a nice bottle of chilled sake, a quart of gin, some juice, and a Ouija board. Cal made way for her to sit on the swing and disappeared into the house for glasses, ice, bean dip, and Fritos. They would be a happy, but gassy, bunch tonight.

As the first stars found a socket to plug into and began to silently wink at the trio, it seemed perfectly natural for the talk to turn to the paranormal. All three had had experiences that couldn't be explained in any logical fashion.

Dixie, who had been scanning Cal's latest edition of *UFO Magazine*, said, "Cal, didn't you tell me that you had seen a UFO somewhere down on the Texas coast one time? Something about some saucer thing swooping down from the sky and you almost having a wreck?"

Cal shot back, "It had absolutely *nothing* to do with those mushrooms, damn it. I swear that every other car on that highway had to pull over, too. It wasn't just me seeing that crazy shit in the sky! And, if you want to get into it, what about that...that...thing on the back of your thigh? Ingrown hair follicle, my ass. That's an alien mark from when they came and took your eggs back as specimens while you were asleep. It's not my first time at the rodeo, you know, missy."

Dixie threw the magazine at Cal's head and they both laughed, and Lefty said he needed to see a man about a horse.

He jumped off the swing at its apex on the inward trajectory and landed next to the door. Proud of his dismount, he opened the screen door and admired the sacred objects with which Cal had surrounded himself. Rich fabrics lined the walls and Oriental and Persian carpets covered the floors. Stacks of books by Crowley, Huxley, Milton, Baudelaire, and Verlaine lined the walls. What little furniture that occupied the front room was mostly covered by piles of old *Daily Texans*, the university's newspaper.

Cal used these newspapers to find out what was going on in town for that particular day or the week, and of course to clip the coupons for free beer. Next to the fireplace was a box that was known as "The Box." It contained every paper and essay Cal had ever written since fourth grade, and each of them was entitled "Man's Inhumanity to Man." He was very proud of these diatribes and would often pull one out at random during a get-together and read it aloud. Lefty grabbed one from the middle and carefully opened the blue cover. Under the repetitive title was something that made Lefty laugh aloud. The thesis for this particular work was: "You can lead an aardvark to battery acid, but you can't make him drink." Obviously, Cal's absurdist views had been around for longer than they had been friends.

Across the hall was another room that held an old Hocus Pocus pinball machine, a foosball table without any balls, and a dartboard. The wall behind the board was pocked by hundreds of holes from errant darts that had strayed from the bull's-eye, most probably on nights when the "crops" had been harvested and the grapes had been stomped.

He used the bathroom and then carefully washed his hands in the sink after finding some soap in the mirror-covered cabinet. This soap had apparently been liberated from a local motel because it was in near-perfect condition and still didn't cover the palm of his hand. He could even read the name of the inn, Skyview Motel, imprinted on its face. He slowly dried his hands, giving the other two plenty of time to finish their discussion. He joined them during an apparent lull in the conservation and quickly changed the subject.

"Hey, Cal. Remember those 'pox parties' our parents used to have when one of us kids in the neighborhood had some kind of weird disease? Every one of us would show up at the poor kid's house and stick to him like glue. Pretty soon after that, we would all have the same thing, only worse sometimes. What did my dad used to call it? 'The Scabietic Mange of the Undead'? They should have made some wild-ass horror movie about those parties featuring a Joe Bob or someone. And, whatever happened to the carolers that used to sing Christmas songs up and down the block every year around the holidays? The men would be drunk as skunks before they even sang a note, and it only got worse from there. I did like them, though. Sort of got you in the mood..."

Dixie had decided she was "in the mood" for some dancing and before Lefty's gibberish became intolerable she suggested they leave. Forgoing the séance with the Ouija board had been Lefty's intention all along and he happily cleared the porch of any festive evidence. The three walked down the steps of the house, past the ancient Vespa scooter lying on its side, climbed into the '64 Ford truck Cal had just finished revitalizing and drove out onto Speedway.

CHAPTER SEVEN

Speedway Drive had gotten its name from people "speeding" out to the racetrack located in Hyde Park back in the early days of Austin, or so he had been told. It was a convenient way to get to the heart of town without taking the interstate. They passed the university, found Congress Avenue, and then made their way to the warehouse district of Old Pecan Street, which was the sixth street north of Town Lake. They pulled into a parking spot and walked up the avenue. There were mostly storage places with a handful of storefronts, a few of which were open only at night and hosted some of the best blues in the Southwest. There were few, if any, white faces here, but all three felt as if this were a kindred reunion. After paying a pittance for entry, they worked their way to the back, warmly greeting friendly faces as they passed. This joint consisted of seven rickety card tables like Cal had in the garage and twenty-one folding chairs. There were only three chairs per table because no one wanted to have his back to the band. The bar was comprised of three long, antique "ice boxes" like one might find in a 1950s gas station outside of Lubbock. There were no lids to these coolers, only bottles of beer with buckets of ice thrown on top to fill the space. It was a dollar fifty for a quart of Schlitz, with a complimentary drinking bag thrown in. Tyler "T. D." Bell from Dime Box, Texas, was on stage and the walls dripped with the sweat of the frenzied crowd. Tonight, there were almost no slow blues numbers, just the barnburners where the band picked up the tempo as the song went along.

After a few hours, Dixie realized that the three of them had not eaten any dinner, and the shaking of her moneymaker was putting her hunger into overdrive. Collecting the few belongings they had brought, they left as they had come, smiling and shaking every extended hand. The night air now seemed to have a nip in it compared to the humidity of the club, and they hurried to the truck, praying it would start. Thankfully, the motor turned over immediately and the friends zoomed home. They said their good-byes on the sidewalk, and Lefty reminded Cal of the Full Moon Party two nights from now at Mickey and Danton's house. This was an affair not to be missed and they promised to talk the next day.

Dixie whipped up her famous King Ranch Chicken and they dined on the porch, watching the moon play hide-and-seek with the clouds.

They both fell asleep as soon as their heads hit the pillows.

The next day passed quietly, and the lawn was given a haircut before an afternoon shower dropped by to leave some needed moisture in the ground. Pancho would arrive tomorrow afternoon, and, thinking of haircuts, Lefty made appointments with his barber for a trim and a shave for them both. He did some laundry and general cleaning before Dixie returned home at dark. Having clean sheets in the guest bedroom was as important to her as breathing, so she was relieved upon her arrival to see that Pancho's sleeping arrangements were in order and he would not be sleeping on soiled linens. Lefty wondered if she had any idea of the filth they had slept in over the years in various countries, but he thought it best not to bring this up, as it might impugn his own hygienic integrity.

While Dixie changed out of her work duds and donned her flame-retardant grilling outfit, Lefty piddled in the kitchen looking for the various ingredients that would compose their salad. He was excited to find fresh basil, tomatoes, celery, and a plump Vidalia onion for crunch, a hard-boiled egg, and four questionable radishes. He cleaned the black spots so Dixie wouldn't be any the wiser as to their blemished appearance and refuse to eat the dish entirely. He gathered them in a large bowl normally reserved for popcorn on rainy nights and, stepping over a snoring Bones, moved carefully to the table. The creak of the old flooring woke the cat and he strutted out the open back door, but not before throwing a perturbed scowl over his shoulder. Lefty returned to the counter for a large wooden cutting board and several pieces of precision cutlery.

Unlike many of his friends, Lefty had no use for guns, but he had always had a fondness for knives, both small and large. They seemed to be more practical for everyday use, a license was not required to own one, and they were easier to maintain. He set up his chopping station near the window so that he might keep an eye on the house pyromaniac and began the ritual of preparing his part of the meal. He relaxed as his hands went through the practiced motions and let his mind wander. Chop, chop, chop. Happy, happy, happy. Chop, chop, chop. Ritual, ritual, ritual. Things were good in his world tonight.

Chapter Eight

She had won him on a small pool table in a cheap bar on the south Texas coast. The table was an old six-footer that needed re-felting and ate two quarters per game. Dixie knew how to handle a pool cue and had been running the table for over an hour before he had thrown open the door to the bar, letting in the scalding radiance of a setting sun.

Sunlight in a windowless bar could bring out the worst in daytime drunks, and even the pinball players in the back yelled their disapproval. Luckily, both the patrons and the new arrival were on an even playing field for the moment, as their eyes adjusted to the change in lighting, and Lefty felt his way to the nearest bar stool. The hoots waned and, recognizing the barkeep, he ordered his usual. As he scanned the police blotter of the freshly printed edition of the weekly rag, he was pleased to find that crime in the area this week was confined to the actions of a few juvenile miscreants stealing bicycles and whatnot. Last week there had been a rash of domestic disturbances (read: drunk wife, drunk husband with an empty net of fish for dinner, screaming children complaining about a lack of bikes to ride, bottles fly, fight ensues, etc...) and two parking tickets had been issued. The tickets were unusual, in that there were no marked parking spots in town and only three fire hydrants. The only "official" spots were for the sheriff and the mayor, reserved and roped off in front of the post office/courthouse, and these were usually empty because their cars were normally parked behind the Sail Club.

Lefty was considering the lawlessness of the area when he felt a tap on his shoulder. He leaped off his stool, only to find an angel standing behind him. Flip-flops instead of sandals and a pool cue instead of a harp, Lefty correctly ascertained that this cherub posed no immediate danger and sheepishly climbed back on his seat.

"You look like you can shake a stick. Wanna play?" Dixie said, flashing a smile.

Lefty, ignorantly thinking he had gained the upper hand, answered, "That might be arranged... What's your name, hon?"

Dixie laughed and turned on her heel, saying only, "You'll just have to find that out, won't you!"

Scooping up the change the barkeep had piled in front of him, Lefty followed her back to the table. "Hey, c'mon. Everybody's got a name. They gotta call you something."

"They call me a lot of things, some that I wouldn't repeat, even in a place like this. But if you're a real good boy, you can call me anytime," she said, looking over her shoulder coyly.

Lefty liked what he saw and could only mutter, "You're *something*, alright."

Two hours later, Lefty found himself back at the bar, alone. She had taken him for a ride and he hadn't wanted to get off. Benji had laid his quarters up while Lefty wasn't looking and had seized the opportunity to play with his angel. Out of luck and out of beer money, much less quarters for pool, he sadly left to make the short walk back to the motel. As he reached the street, the padded front door squeaked open and the neon light of too many beer signs chased his shadow away. He heard tiny footfalls in his wake and turned to find a luminescent halo following him. She extended her hand and said, "You forgot something." He looked down to find a Tecate coaster with a phone number hurriedly scribbled in eyeliner pencil.

Dixie looked up at Lefty and stammered out awkwardly, "I only came down for a few days to get a little sun, you know, and the weather just isn't cooperating very well, at least in the afternoons, so…well, I was just wondering, if you aren't doing anything in the next day or two and you want to lose a little more money, I've got another game I play. It's called nine-ball and it really is a lot of—"

Lefty interrupted her, saying, "Hey, you ever flown a kite?"

The next days were a blur of laughter and rolling on the beach, without a second thought to ever playing nine-ball, for they had found a new game much more to their liking. They left the island together and would not be apart from each other for any length of time again. He had never felt this way about another person in his life. They shared the same goals, education, sense of humor, and character. Dixie was at least as outgoing as he was, if not more, and quite quick to laugh. They enjoyed doing the same things and knew where the right buttons to push were located. They supported each other as only a loving, devoted couple could, and relied on one another's advice when needed. Then there was the lovemaking—that was something else. And to this day, he never again saw a kite soaring on the wind without a halo attached to it.

Lefty enjoyed the memory and resumed his chopping. Out of the corner of his eye, he spied a large but controlled fireball erupting from the Weber grill, singeing the lower branches of the mimosa tree directly overhead. Dixie began the ritualistic fire dance as their two black cats raced for the safety of a darkened alley. As the dance became more frenzied, his chopping speed increased, and within a few minutes an appetizing salad presented itself. Proud of his creation, he pulled out the plate of thick T-bones that had been resting in the fridge and shuffled outside in his bare feet. Dixie sat on top of the picnic table next to the fire; having assumed a strange yoga position, she stared at the sparkling flames. Not wanting to interrupt her trance, Lefty placed the slabs of beef next to her and retreated to the warm kitchen, licking off the garlic and pepper that crusted his fingers as he went.

He walked into the library after checking the mail and placed the lone postcard from his Uncle Ben on the table next to his reading chair. It was posted from somewhere in Laos, where he was stationed as what was vaguely described as a cultural attaché. He had been away for a long time and it was always good to hear from him. Lefty decided he would read the card in the morning with the rising sun. He put on some acceptable dinner music and returned outside to the smell of the charcoal burning nicely.

The dying flames had broken the spell and Dixie unfolded herself from the yoga pyramid. She found her favorite pair of tongs and quickly set to work finishing the more mundane part of the fire process—the actual grilling. Soon, the steaks were ready; his still mooing, hers almost shoe leather. The cats, smelling meat, cautiously crept back to the house and curled up under the table at their feet. After adding a fresh basil vinaigrette to the salad, they dined and enjoyed each other's company without a care in the world.

Fully sated, the dishes were placed in the sink to soak, and after a grape Popsicle melted on their lips, they climbed the stairs and slipped between the cool sheets. They fell asleep to a soothing concerto on the radio and did not wake until dawn.

The next day, Dixie decided not to take the day off after all, but promised to be home by five p.m. She had festooned the porch with banners and glitter balloons ready to welcome their dear comrade. After she left the house, Lefty cleared the breakfast dishes and cleaned the cat bowls. He slid into an overly comfortable chair and again perused his "bible." Had he forgotten anything? He decided he had done a pretty fair job and gazed out the window. The better angels of his unconscious mind told him not to worry, that somehow everything was going to be alright. This comforted him and he put the notebook away.

There was an abrupt knock on the door just before it blew open to reveal an enormous hulk of humanity. Pancho had arrived in all his glory, wearing brightly colored pantaloons and a Mexican wedding shirt with the sleeves unbuttoned. Across his chest were two bandoliers that caused Lefty to look around nervously for a shotgun. His head was covered by a titanic sombrero and he appeared to be shoeless.

"Pumpernickel, I am here, *GODDAMN IT*! I have just driven at top speed from Piedras Negras bringing supplies, and made it all the way to the outskirts of Austin before I even laid eyes on old Johnny Law, who was just waiting to stop me one more time and lock me up in County for 'conduct unbecoming.' But *nooo*! I could not and would not let that pesky little warrant stand between us and our date with infamy. I promise you, we will not be deterred on this one, my friend. No, no, no, no, *no*! I have come prepared, expecting the best, but planning for the worst. I tell you, I feel alive! This is it. The one we have waited for! I tell you, I am so jazzed, I don't know whether I'm coming or going. Where's my drink? Nah, fuck caffeine. I am on a *natural high*! I can feel it flowing through my veins already, leaping up into my skull and bouncing around looking for a place to land."

Lefty collapsed in the nearest chair trying to stay out of his friend's way. Pancho was indeed alive and storming around the bottom floor of the house like a tornado. In his excited state of mind, he would appear in various doorways, sticking his head in one and back through another. He was in the middle of a full blown adrenaline rush and Lefty was exhausted just watching his antics. And how in the hell had he recalled Lefty's childhood nickname, Pumpernickel, during this emotional exhibition?

"I tell you, this will be the trip of a lifetime and we shall cut no corners," Pancho continued. "It will be full-tilt boogie all the way to heaven from here on out. I will not close my eyes for one *momentito*, for fear I might not awaken and miss the journey entirely. *No, sir!* I shall not rest from here on out. I just want to..."

Lefty interrupted his good friend and threatened to call the cops if he did not settle down. Like a balloon, Pancho deflated from head to toe, turned, grabbed Lefty by the shoulders, and said, "But, I digress..."

They embraced as usual, with Pancho nearly crushing Lefty's spine. He retreated to the

Oldsmobile convertible parked at the curb and grabbed his solid-body Halliburton aluminum suitcase from the backseat. As he did so, he noticed smoke emerging from the hood. Lefty joined him on the sidewalk and helped survey the situation. Pancho raised the hood and was enveloped in a cloud of angry steam. "Perhaps you should have had the engine checked before you left the border, my friend," was all that Lefty could say.

A jogger slowed as he passed the two and asked if the car had broken down. Lefty looked at Pancho and then back to the runner. Both realized at the same time that they were looking at the new president of the "Apostle of the Obvious Club, Austin Chapter," and the two friends broke up in laughter. Shooing the jogger away, Lefty led Pancho back to the house and let him find the way to his old room. He returned soon with more news of his adventures and the two quickly fell into the rhythm of their friendship so like the lifelong pals they were.

The yin and yang between the two made them complementary in many ways. For instance, Pancho was always a "Zeppelin" while Lefty was a "Beatle." When they were just learning about the world of music, virtually everyone fit into one of these two camps. "Zeps" were a mystical, spiritual group while "Beats" were playful and full of life. The other polarizing characteristic to their natures was that Pancho was always the life of the party, or the entertainment, and Lefty was the party giver. He threw parties often and enjoyed every minute of it, particularly the planning and preparation, which fit nicely with his ritualistic side.

They caught up on things and Pancho was secretive about his Mexican purchases, but promised to explain later. Their conversation was interrupted by a howling from the front yard. Looking out the large bay windows, they discovered a lunatic on the grass, thrashing and flailing like a dervish. Pancho immediately recognized this imbecile as Cal and ran out the front door. Cal had recognized the car and, in his usual way, had decided to welcome his old friend to the neighborhood. They danced an odd jig around the lawn before regaining their senses and returned to the relative sanity of the house. Pancho wondered aloud about finding a mechanic while Cal thought of reasons not to. Cal grabbed the sombrero that was, amazingly, still on Pancho's head and donned it at a tilt. "Argh, matey! How ye be? I'm as good a mechanic as ye will find in these parts and I am off for the day." They all laughed again and agreed it was time to hit Dry Creek Saloon and visit Sarah.

Cal's truck could probably find its way to Mount Bonnell by itself in a hailstorm. The trick was coaxing it up the final leg of the steep cliff. Mount Bonnell was famous as a place for university students to "park," and it was indeed a beautiful place to do it. Narrow trails led off in various directions from the peak where, at the ends, there would be collections of beer cans and condom wrappers, a final landing pad for the not-so-lonely-heart crew. At night, one could see stars and other celestial sights that were not visible in other points of the city. Located at the very top and with breathtaking views of Lake Austin was Dry Creek Saloon, workplace of the churlish Sarah. To say it was a bar proper would be an insult to the dreariest of dives. The truck chugged its way up the mountain and slid into the only parking spot available.

This was a popular hangout on spring afternoons for many reasons. Besides being able to look down at the lake almost eight hundred feet below, there was plenty of cheap cold beer, picnic tables to stretch out on, and, of course, pickled pig's feet and boiled eggs. Almost no one sat inside; instead, most chose to climb up to the deck on the roof and admire nature. But before making it upstairs, you had to get past the hard-boiled bartender, Sarah. She was tougher than a nickel steak with a glare that could bore through your soul like a laser. You had to be polite when ordering and at least feign some interest in the pickled offerings. When reordering, you would be scolded and refused service if the empties were not returned, if you considered a verbal hurricane of foul language to be a scolding.

Pancho ordered three Carta Blancas—rather appropriate considering his current outfit—wrapped them in one of his Herculean paws and led the way upstairs. They spread out at one of the tables under a speaker that would provide the soundtrack for the afternoon, and during the next few hours caught up on the activities of the others while enjoying the un-cloudy day.

"Pancho, you still pulling the day shift at that savings and loan you were always jabbering about?" Cal asked, between gulps of the Mexican *cerveza*. "I was thinking I might need some walking-around money for a little project I got in mind."

Pancho sniffed a particularly malodorous overly pickled egg, tossed it over the railing, and said, "Nope. And I'm never going back there, ever. Something's a little fishy about that place and my radar's up. Don't know what it is and I don't *want* to know. It feels like everybody's looking over their shoulder at goblins. I told them I was moving on to greener pastures in the animal husbandry field. Shocked the shit out of 'em, alright. But I just had to get out. And I suppose you two characters are still in the soup lines, hmmm? You've never had a job as long as I've known you, Cal, and as for you, my little yellow friend, just picking up the classifieds gives you the willies. What did it say on that important-looking business card you had drawn up—probably in crayon, I might add—something like Corporate Efficiency Expert? Biggest crock of shit I've ever heard...should have been Expert Village Idiot or something."

Lefty was smiling and taking all of this in when a low-flying buzzard dropped a perfect three-pointer directly into the throat of his longneck bottle. This was a cause for great hilarity and joking for a solid minute or two.

"I think that's our cue," Lefty finally said, standing and checking his hair for other droppings.

"Oh, *noooo*, pal!" Pancho replied. "I think that sent us into overtime. Besides, I still haven't heard those songs I played for my gal, Sarah."

Lefty once again took his seat and said, "Hey, while we're talking about *dinero*, I have an idea we might want to think about. I know of a casino-type joint over off Congress where we might get a little pocket money for the trip. Nothing big, you know, just a little something to keep our boat afloat, just in case. Wouldn't take a lot of time or skill, just in and out...easy money, I hear. Course, I said that about the Cowboys in Super Bowl Five. That's why I hate the city of Miami. Never liked it then or since. Goddamn field goal kickers—they all ought to be shot. Thought Landry was going to have a 'come to Jesus' fit and meet our maker right then and there. Anyway, what do you think, Pancho?"

Pancho retorted, "If I had all the money that you've lost betting on football over the years, I'd be living in a hut in Bora-Bora with ten nekkid women."

When they were all sufficiently sun-kissed, the three lumbered down the stairs, dropped the bottles on the bar and climbed into the truck. The trip back home would be much more fun because it was all downhill and you could coast in neutral all the way. The trick was trying not to hit the brakes at all until you got back to the main road. They narrowly survived the idiocy of this undertaking and made it home in good time.

After a few more beers, Lefty decided he needed a power nap before this evening's festivities. Pancho grabbed a bag from his room that looked suspiciously like it had originated south of the border, took out a small container, put the bag back in the hall closet, and joined Cal and Bones on the porch before heading next door. It seemed that Pancho had indeed brought along his "party favors," but was still keeping the stash to himself. Lefty watched from the bedroom window and saw the black flag slowly rise up the pole, followed by the garage door creaking closed.

Lefty was refreshed when he awoke, and took his cold shower. He pulled on some fairly clean jeans, a denim shirt, and deck shoes without socks. He headed downstairs and put on some music to go with his mood. He had always used music to set the tone for specific occasions...or for no occasion at all. Music for rain, holidays, the beach, even sleep, was at his fingertips there in his wonderful library. Tonight, the music would be in honor of a brilliant full moon and it would be Van "The Man" Morrison's ethereal *Moondance*. He carefully wiped the disc and balanced it atop the spindle, ready to be dropped at the appropriate time. The "occasion" tonight was the full moon and the party that always accompanied it. It would also be a sort of going-away party for Lefty and Pancho, and would be a night to remember for many reasons. But, the most important one was that this would be the last time their friends would see them as "virgins."

He opened all of the downstairs windows and let the aroma of the fragrant mimosas fill the afternoon air. Placing some nicely scented candles on the front porch, he noticed a leaf that had found its way onto the porch so he pushed a broom around for a bit, all the while wondering what was going on next door. He didn't have long to wait, as Dixie jolted into the driveway, again on two wheels, and honked her horn. His buddies must have gotten the message because they soon emerged from the garage. Led by Bones, they climbed the steps and greeted Dixie.

"Look at you! I can't believe it. You made it in one piece this time and not a scar on you. At least not on the parts I can see. *Oh, boy!* Lefty's been a bundle of nerves ever since he got your letter." Dixie wore a grin that spanned the sky.

All Lefty could think was, *What? Me, a bundle of nerves? You should have seen this crazy wildcat a few hours ago...*

Hardly able to contain himself, Pancho responded, "Hey, Dixie! It's great to see you, too. It has been *waaaay* too long. You still the house pyromaniac? I got something real nice for you from just across the border. All you need, my dear, are the matches! But be careful. They aren't what you call legal around here. Give me a second, you hear?"

She squealed with glee and threw her arms around his muscular neck. He spun her around like a ribbon on a maypole and everyone clapped like wind-up monkeys smacking cymbals together. Pancho ventured into the house, returning with the gifts and a devilish smile.

Cal's darker side was well pleased when he received a riding crop and a ten-foot leather bullwhip from the border "goodie bag." Cal had always had a keen eye for what was au courant with his type of "lady," and these might be useful for the upcoming weekend with his Asian gal.

Next, Pancho handed Lefty a bag that contained a stuffed frog playing a guitar and, wrapped in a kerchief, something very special indeed. It was an authentic Native American rattle, used by medicine men to heal the sick, bring rain, or drive out evil spirits. This also might come in handy in the next few days, and Lefty proudly placed it on the mantel.

Later, the boys dressed and then waited while Dixie finished getting ready. Excited, the three poured shots of the *anejo* into thin, tall glasses and enjoyed the tartness of the key limes. A warm glow from the aged tequila slowly enveloped them as they awaited the arrival of tonight's guest of honor. The guest of honor, or moon, arrived about twenty minutes later in a blaze of glory. More brilliant yellow than white, at least for the moment, it slowly ascended skyward. With Mr. Moon having arrived at his event, it was time to mosey down the street to Mickey and Danton's, where this month's party would be held.

Mickey and Danton had been friends to them all from back in the old days. They lived just a few blocks away in the close-knit and free-thinking neighborhood of Hyde Park and saw each other often. It was said that they had been the originators of these monthly fests, but Lefty surmised otherwise. He had read of moon celebrations in Native American lore and these fit nicely with his penchant for ritual and ceremony.

When they approached the house, they saw a collection of cars filling the driveway, yard, and street. They found the nearest ladder and climbed aboard. The roof was alive with shadowed forms, some dancing, some drinking, and all were laughing. They headed toward the makeshift bar and got in what appeared to be the line. Lefty recognized the fellow in front of him immediately and they shook hands warmly. This was Bill, and the first thing out of his mouth was a warning to be careful of the punch, something about a "Mexican Special" being served tonight. Lefty turned to see Pancho rocking on his heels with an ear-to-ear grin on his tanned face smiling back at him. Bill had a distinct cherry-red stain circling his lips, and from the appearance of his eyes, he seemed to know what he was talking about. The two had been roommates for years and Lefty had never seen him in this shape. He was enjoying himself fully, and Lefty itched to move ahead and check it out.

Bill stuck his chin in the air as if admiring his visage in a mirror and said, "I've got a few zits, but I'm not concerned."

Lefty looked around to see if this cryptic announcement was directed at someone else. Nobody answered this...this...whatever it might have been. Some form of self-confident testimonial, perhaps? A warning of sorts? Leaving Lefty to shrug his shoulders and slowly say, "Yes. I think I understand...the punch. It's the punch. I'll watch out for it."

He finally made it to the self-serve bar, poured two cups of the concoction, and handed them to Dixie. He then poured two more for himself and relinquished his spot to Cal. Cal, having been in on the brewing of this special batch, cautiously took a small sip, let it roll around on his tongue, gauged its strength, and began barking like a dog. Lefty assumed this was a good sign and watched Cal pour an oversized glass for himself. Pancho chugged his first cup and then had a refill.

They moved around the roof to see who was in attendance and found Danton surrounded by a group of lovelies. He broke from them when he saw his old friends, and was a whirlwind of animated speech, arms flailing in the air and hands mimicking sign language like all good Italians do. Lefty's suspicions about the punch were proven to be true when Danton repeatedly and profusely thanked Pancho for his "special" contribution. Lefty, remembering Pancho's nefarious tete-a-tete with Cal earlier during his nap, eyed his punch warily, and then, seeing that Dixie had already finished her first cup and was nursing a second, swallowed the first gulp.

The punch had a musty, almost mushroom-y, taste but was enjoyable other than that. Danton thought it was time to catch up with the other guests, so he threw an arm around Lefty's shoulder and asked that he accompany him around. They seemed to know almost everyone there. All were dancing to the new cassette stereo and watching the lunar extravaganza. Girls twirled in the moonlight doing a free-form dance to the gods. Danton managed to get the attention of one of the girls and was gone for the nonce.

Lefty noticed a particular character in the back of the crowd who seemed to levitate above the others. She resembled a Disney wizard, wearing a long pointed hat and some form of cloak or topcoat that was gathered at the collar like it was somehow pinned there. She watched over the dancers with delight until her eyes met Lefty's, when they narrowed and squinted at him for a moment. She leaned back like she was ready to throw a changeup and hurled a fireball the size of a cantaloupe at his chest. It landed with an explosion of sparks and knocked Lefty backward, his hands grasping his sternum. His fingertips were scorched somewhat but did not hurt. This shocked him for a moment, until he remembered the "spiked" Mexican punch. Stars of bright colors remained, not in his eyes, but in his actual being. Everything was electric with energy, and it was not a bad feeling at all. Dixie, noticing her husband's bewilderment, arrived at his side to reassure him that things would be okay. They rejoined the group, with Lefty's body still tingling, and found a seat near the edge of the roof. He looked over his shoulder to see what had become of this "wizard" and saw only the swirling dancers keeping time to the music. He felt a sense of loss at her disappearance, but quickly chalked it up to the beverage. Dixie was feeling daring and had swung her legs over the gutter by now. Regaining some semblance of normalcy and not wanting another incident to happen on this fine evening, he pulled her up and into his lap. The two nuzzled for what seemed like ages before heading to the dance floor. They were having so much fun that they lost track of time, several hours in fact, and when they looked around most everyone had gone downstairs or left. They unsteadily descended the now-wobbly ladder and made their way to the patio.

The food that Danton had put out earlier was mostly gone, but some fine gumbo and bread were left. Lefty knew his way around a kitchen, but Danton was a master at everything culinary, particularly seafood and barbecue.

After a quick cleanup by the four friends, they bid Danton adieu and walked out the front door. There, sitting on the hood of his car, were Mickey and the second-prettiest girl around. Lefty had not seen him all night and now he knew why.

"Get a room, why don't you? There are laws about that sort of thing around here!" Cal shouted sarcastically. Mickey's girl du jour giggled. Her mammoth naked breasts literally jiggled and she grew bashful, so, with practiced hands, she readjusted her lacy brassiere and wandered away, leaving the others to chat.

Dixie teased, "Hey, Mick, don't wipe off that lipstick. It looks like it's your color! Jungle Red, I believe." What appeared to be a giant group grope ensued that led to the ostentatious announcement of Lefty and Pancho's upcoming "passage" by Cal.

"Yeah, I heard something about that," Mickey said. "In fact, the whole neighborhood was gossiping about it today. I think someone has already started a bail fund for you two knuckleheads, just in case. I think the last time y'all got in deep with the law was when you were on one of your adventures to—"

Lefty interrupted and droned, "Yeah, yeah. Move along, Johnny, there's nothing to see here. And speaking of knuckleheads, why in the hell did you let that gal slip away so easily? She had the ideal 'hitch in her get-along,' if you get what I'm saying. Sorry we missed seeing you tonight, but I see you had your hands full—both of them, in fact. Dixie's getting a little bushed and we should take our leave, so just don't take any wooden Indians while we're gone."

The group waved good-bye and made their way into the night. As they neared his home, Lefty noticed a lone figure at the end of the driveway. It was Bones, observing all the action. He followed the group back to the porch where they lit candles and collapsed into the rockers. By this time, the moon was almost as high in the sky as they were. Lefty looked at his fingertips and found that there were black scorch marks on them. He remembered the wizard incident and wondered if she had cast a spell on him, then shrugged it off. Cal had dozed off with a familiar devilish smile on his face. Lefty, knowing that he was to meet Annie the next day for lunch at Threadgill's, suggested they call it a night. He found a quilt, draped it over Cal, and blew out the candles one by one. Pancho seemed to be full of energy, and crossed the street to see if Townes was home, with Pinkie at his heels.

Lefty turned on the dishwasher and followed Dixie upstairs, watching her undress in the moonlight. She was a striking girl and he liked to watch her doing the simplest things, especially undressing. She chose one of his white long-sleeved shirts and a pair of socks, and then pulled back the cool, soft sheets. She slipped into the comfort of the imported cotton, wiggled her fingers at him in a wave, and closed her eyes. Before he followed her to dreamland, Lefty heard the slow *whoosh... whoosh...whoosh* of the dishwasher downstairs and the faint whistle of the twelve-thirty northbound Katy chugging past the railroad crossings nearby, and thought about a girl from Colorado...

CHAPTER

NINE

Annie Globes and Lefty had been childhood friends. They had spent many summers together at Barton Springs enjoying the sun and the scenery. She was a girl of uncommon beauty, intellect, and wit. They enjoyed each other's company so much that they, at some point, had become inseparable. During puberty, they spent many a long night talking on the phone trying to decipher the secrets of the opposite sex. In their high school years, they would often go to sock hops and barn dances, dancing through the night and sometimes even holding hands. This would cause his hormones to react at inopportune times and she would help with his embarrassment by excusing herself to find the bathroom. When she returned, she would grab him and lead him to the dance floor where they would slow dance, which of course only exasperated the situation for Lefty. Looking back, he realized she had enjoyed her hold over men in general, and him in particular. It would become a permanent character trait for her, yet Lefty knew he had a friend for life. He was sad when she decided to attend college in the high country, a place she would never tire of, but they continued to regularly correspond on holidays and birthdays through the years.

On those occasions when they were able to speak, he learned she was now a very different person than he remembered. She had more than blossomed into a voluptuous woman and was hairless from the ears down. With these new attributes, she had attracted more attention from men than she had ever wanted and had been through quite a few bad relationships. It had inured her from getting involved with another male on a regular basis, with the one exception of a nomadic mountain man she had discovered altogether by accident. Several times a year, this wayfaring soul would venture down below the tree line bringing gifts to her. They would disappear for days into a rustic cabin and not emerge again until they were both fully sated. During these interludes, animalistic grunts and howls would ring through the brittle night air, followed by what sounded like the walloping of leather against bare skin. He would disappear as energetically as he had arrived, and always under the cover of night. She would return to her life on the mountain, tending to her children and relishing life. Her "children" were wounded or handicapped animals she had come upon during her daily walks and taken in to nurse back to health. She had found her calling and seemed to be quite content.

She strolled into Threadgill's like a mirage in the midday sun and was dripping in sexuality and turquoise jewelry. She found her friend sitting at a table near the rear and slid into the red vinyl booth. Just like with Pancho, they quickly fell into their comradeship and talked nonstop for almost an hour, shooing away the waiter each time he returned to fill the enormous tea glasses. They relived the earlier days of innocence and joked that nothing had really changed between them. He still loved her, but in a much different way than before. He had found his muse in Dixie, who knew what buttons to push and when, while Annie just knew where the buttons were. She could dance the dance of the flirt and hold him with her eyes and fingers, but that was all. The naughty things that leaked from her tongue caressed his crotch from a distance, flicking, nibbling, and teasing his manhood to attention, which then slowly drooped with the arrival of the unwelcome waiter. She was his "whimsy" where Dixie was his "ritual." He had always cherished her deep laugh and today was no different. It was never a fake cackle or a titter, and he appreciated that greatly. Looking at her, he recognized the value of a true friendship where there was no judgment or appraisal.

She asked how Dixie was and this sparked another hour-long discourse, this time in between bites of food, as they were both famished. The meal was remarkable again today, but was not the center of attention because of the special connection they shared.

The day passed far too quickly for both of them and, seeing that they were the only folks left in the dining room, they decided it was time for the check. They fought over who would pay, and as usual she was relentless. They both knew he would slip her three fins when she wasn't looking, so they walked out happy, with her arm over his shoulder. They wandered back to her truck and sat in the cab.

"Annie, why do you always run away so soon? I mean, you just got here and all we did was conduct business. Barton is just up the street and we could see if Marta would let us sit in that lifeguard stand way at the end, just like we used to."

Annie looked forward and threw her blonde hair across her face, leaving only one eye to peer through the strands. That same Cyclopsian eye moved slowly to face him and she said shyly, "My mother taught me never to socialize with Episcopalians." This had become her standard answer to all things Lefty and they both cracked up, beaming at the tired justification.

She passed him a cigar box containing the peyote in exchange for an envelope containing his payment. "You watch out, you hear me? I'm not going to be running down here to bail you out of the can again. I think that's somebody else's job now..."

He had forgotten about the time in high school when some misfits had corralled him into setting fire to a few book lockers in a back hallway. Instead of burning, they had just melted in front of their eyes like candles in the wind. And to top it off, it was *his* locker that was reduced to a molten heap of scrap metal. Annie had been the one to send him his "Get Out of Jail Free" card that afternoon, when his parents had decided to see how long it would take for him to get used to rations of hardtack and gruel.

They hugged for a time before he reached for the handle. He had always hated good-byes, so just winks and smiles were exchanged between the two. He closed the heavy door and she pulled out of the lot. He looked down to his hand and found the crumpled bills he had forgotten to hide in her pocket. She had done it again.

C H A P T E R
T E N

Lefty returned from lunch, only to find Pancho waiting for him on the high front porch. Lefty had completely forgotten about the appointment with Verne, the barber, and was scolded for it. The two quickly made their way to the Goodall-Wooten Barbershop and slipped into the relaxing chairs. Lefty had been coming to see Verne for many years and he was not too fussy about their tardiness.

Verne was an effeminate German man who spoke in tones so low that you had to concentrate hard not only to hear, but then to decipher his thick accent. He lived a few miles away in the small German enclave of New Braunfels. He loved to hunt and fish, and always offered pieces of homemade jerky instead of candy like the other barbers of Lefty's childhood. Verne liked to tell the story of his "legendary" barber chair, where he claimed that Charles Whitman had actually shot the customer who was sitting in it getting a trim during the infamous University of Texas Tower massacre. Lefty did not know whether to believe him, but it made for a good story, and Lefty was soon fast asleep.

Verne was famous for giving a Swedish massage when he finished, and it was always so relaxing that Lefty often made an appointment even when he didn't need a decent whacking. And it was most certainly cheaper that the massage parlors along the interstate, even without the "happy final release."

. After their shaves and cuts, the two headed south to pick up the last item needed to complete the shopping list. Turning onto the 1600 block of Lavaca, Lefty saw the sign above the store shining in the afternoon sun. Capitol Saddlery was the finest maker of handmade leather goods and horse tack in the country. The Steiner family had been the owner/operators of this wonderful Western store since the 1930s. Buck ran the register up front and was genial enough, but the real magic happened in the back, where a smallish man cobbled the finest and most comfortable boots known to man. He—The Beret— never went anywhere without his French cap, was quick with your name, and was widely acknowledged as the grandest raconteur this side of Hondo Crouch.

Hondo was famous for being the owner of Luckenbach, Texas, population three, where he proclaimed himself Governor of the Dance Hall. The Washer Finals were held there every May and

Hondo was known throughout the Southwest for his storytelling abilities. He held the rapt attention of children huddled around campfires with tales about things that go bump in the night and talking deer. Stories came alive when he opened his mouth, and he always ended his yarns with a cliffhanger ending, leaving the audience clamoring for more. In many ways, he and The Beret were local legends.

The Beret's name was Charlie Dunn and, true to his Irish heritage, he enjoyed a brew once and again. He was a true iconoclast in every sense of the word and embodied the term "colorful Texan." He had earned and deserved great riches in his lifetime, but like Hondo, had chosen not the riches of wealth but the treasures of life. Lefty had bought his footwear from Hondo at the Saddlery for many years and was currently in need of a resoling on his traveling boots. He had also long ago adopted their minimalist philosophy of life, but the best tonic for wanderlust was a trustworthy pair of leather stitching on your feet, and he would happily cough up the cost on the strength of the "trustworthy" part alone.

Entering the tall front doors, the two friends' nostrils were filled with the aroma of all things leather—a smell known to every good Texan. Nodding to Buck as they passed, they walked down the long aisles running their fingers over the saddles, purses, and bridles on their way to the double doors that led to the workroom in the rear. Eying them as they walked through the doors, Charlie reached under the counter, pulled out a paper sack containing Lefty's manly foot-wear, and handed him a bill and a beer.

"Looks like somebody got *all* of their hairs cut today," Charlie said, removing the beret. Stroking his bald pate, he said softly, almost to himself, "I'm not real sure I even know where a *true* barber keeps shop these days. All those damn stylists running around in girly clothes and hats acting like they're the Queen of England or something."

He found his stool and sat, only to stand again and retrieve his beer. He was in a good mood today and it made for a fine afternoon. Stories were related and lies told for the better part of an hour before Charlie said Cecile was probably ringing the dinner bell at home. He walked the two to the door, making sure the pair had Lefty's retreads in hand. It never struck Lefty as odd that he didn't even think to inspect the craftsmanship; he didn't need to. Some things and some people were above reproach. Now, with the last of the shopping completed, they left with a warm feel-ing of family and found their way home, knowing they would soon embark on the trip of a lifetime.

CHAPTER ELEVEN

Austin was an unusually fun place after dark. Music was everywhere and electricity filled the air. Lefty finished his grooming with a double splash of witch hazel and pulled on his Spanish boots. This pair was the fanciest of his collection and only worn when he needed to make an impression, and tonight at the poker game he would need to make a *large* impression. He joined Pancho on the porch and took a seat across from him. On the table were two brandy snifters, a carafe of tap water, an ice bucket boosted from the Villa Capri, and a bottle of absinthe that Pancho had shipped back to the states in a box claiming to hold mineral water.

Absinthe was a distilled, highly alcoholic drink popular in Europe until the 1920s, when it was claimed to be highly addictive and therefore a danger to society. Hallucinations were common and reality was said to shift and change like the sands in the desert. Things would appear suddenly and just morph away into the ether. It was of interest to the two because of its bohemian connotations and the inherent danger. Lefty was particularly curious, as it was defined as a "spirit" rather than a liqueur and there was that special something he craved that accompanied drinking it—a ritual.

There was a procedure to follow when consuming this delicacy, one that Lefty had never been a party to, and so naturally Pancho took the reins. He assumed a very impressive and learned look on his face as he pulled a silver spoon from his leather vest and arranged the needed implements to begin the ceremony. The flat, slotted spoon was placed across the rim of one of the glasses containing the absinthe and a sugar cube was positioned on top of it. He carefully rolled up his shirtsleeves, took hold of the carafe, and slowly began to drip water over the sugar until the cube had dissolved. He repeated these steps with the second snifter and then set the water down. He rolled his sleeves back into place and sat back to wait on the all-important change of color. When this miracle occurred, he leaned over the table and grabbed three cubes of ice for each glass. Each piece tinkled as it hit the crystal sides. This was not part of the European ceremony, but, this being Texas, ice was added to everything. They slowly began to sip, enjoying the glow provided by the illegal Green Fairy, or *la fée verte*, as it was known across the pond, and worked out a plan of action for the evening.

"Pancho, I was kind of thinking that we don't really need to—"

"Damn it, there you go again, trying to spoil everything with that stinkin' thinkin'," Pancho spat out.

It wasn't that he was really mad at Lefty; it was just his way of saying, "Don't ruin a good thing, numbskull." They had already procured the buttons, or "flesh of the gods" as it was called out West, and done the preparation. It would be impossible to stop at this juncture. This was something that *had* to be done.

"Every time you try and think something out, we end up in trouble. Remember that time, when we were just kids, that time we snuck out the window of that old house you grew up in and tried to jump in that crazy lady's pool with no clothes on? No, no, no! Not the old lady without any clothes on. Us! Can you imagine seeing her nekkid? Oh, God. Anyway, your mom caught us going out the window and started screaming something about how she thought it was a burglar. Next thing you know, she's pulling us downstairs by the short hairs to face your father, and he starts yelling about the communists and Castro and all kinds of other crazy shit. He takes us outside saying he is going to beat the hell out of us because that's the way his father handled such things. And once we were out there in the back, he just smiled and said what idiots we were because we got caught and we hadn't even done anything yet! I'll never forget as long as I live what he said next: 'never say boo-hoo when boo will do.' I'm not really sure if that made sense to you then, either, but it makes perfect sense now."

After processing the absurdity of his statement, Pancho sat upright in the chair, threw back his shoulders, and asked, "Shall we dance?" A handshake sealed the deal, and as the drinks began to fully take effect, they stood and surveyed the situation. All clear. They dashed down the steps and into the crisp spring night.

A near-full moon was again high in the sky and brilliant. This was not unusual for Austin, as the city planners had erected very tall towers complete with lights that replicated moonlight each night of the year. This followed the "Keep Austin Weird" edict and Lefty had always found it soothing. With the double dose of moonlight, they hurried down to the Continental Club and found two seats near the door.

The Thunderbirds took the stage as the boys' drinks arrived and the small club became a bundle of nervous energy. The walls shook as the band started the set with a rollicking cover of "My Babe." After a few songs, Lefty looked at his compadre's eyes and noticed that his pupils were the size of two large marbles. He was taking in anything and everything. His smile was only interrupted when his enormous tongue leaped out and wet his lips. Normally, Lefty would find this compelling enough, but his attention was drawn to a dwarf who had approached their table wearing what appeared to be children's clothing. He motioned to Lefty with his stubby fingers to follow him. Lefty stared incredulously at him for what seemed like several minutes. What could this small person possibly want from them? Pancho had become aware of this menace, so he slowly and cautiously reached down to his boot and found the giant handle of the Bowie he had stowed there. Just then, the door flew open and Wyn danced into the room. The dwarf was gone in a flash and Lefty relaxed.

Wyn was a local bon vivante who relished the Austin nightlife and all that accompanied it. She was escorted by a crew of rough-looking characters of whom she was fond and immediately hit the dance floor. She was a whirlwind of motion as she clicked her heels around her companions. She noticed Lefty and threw him a wave. He grabbed it with one hand and returned it with the other. After the song finished and the band took a break, she made her way to the table and greeted Pancho warmly. Lefty hugged her with such force that he momentarily thought he had broken her spine. Her mongrel horde was brusquely shooed away until the business had been concluded. The funds needed for their seats in the big game were exchanged on trust and would be repaid shortly. Having their stake, the two friends slid out of the club and proceeded up Congress Avenue. It was only nine blocks to the game and they couldn't walk quickly enough.

CHAPTER TWELVE

Mr. Bean was standing under the lamppost that lit their meeting place. It was two doors down from the gaming house where, hopefully, the pair would win additional "mad money" for their journey. Lefty made the introduction to Pancho and all three turned to look at the imposing house on the hill.

Lefty had first met Mr. Bean years before. At that time, he was just known as Mike. He had worked for Lefty for many years as a "street consultant," a flippant occupation that he had engraved on business cards that he carried with him in a small leather case. His habit of freely distributing these cards to everyone he met was pure promotional genius. By his mid-teens, he was known as the go-to guy around town. He could rustle up some women for fun, some music for dancing, and special party favors for those so inclined. He was by no means nefarious; he was merely a broker of sorts. Knowledge of this type was a great commodity to possess and he used it well—and to his advantage.

Lefty and Mike were alike in that neither was willing to compromise his freedom or values for the sake of another ne'er-do-well. They simply helped ease the process—a little grease here, a little grease there—just moving things along. His most important attribute, the one Mike was known for, was his honesty. He was positively one of the best men Lefty had ever known.

They had become friends and shared barbe-cues and good times. Mike was one of the few black men to ever invite Lefty into his home to enjoy an evening. His children were a delight and they all shared Mike's blinding smile. They would gather around Lefty's legs as he arrived and check his pockets for the sour candies that always accompanied him.

All of Mike's children, although different in their own ways, were as sweet as summer rain and he relished their company. For some strange reason, he had become known as Uncle Rooroo. This might have arisen from Lefty's obsession with freight trains and his habit of wearing an engineer's cap while manning a grill. As the ribs and chicken were pulled off the fire, Lefty would make a motion like doing a one-armed pull-up, just like an engineer pulling out of the station, and declare, "Roo-roo!"

In his capacity as a street consultant, Mr. Bean would provide them with their entrée to the big poker game. He cautioned them to play it straight and not take too many chances. He asked how much they were looking to win and Lefty said not much, maybe only two big pots' worth. Mr. Bean said he could easily float them the money, to be repaid at their leisure, and then they would not be taking a chance on losing it all. Both Lefty and Pancho had been free of self-doubt all their lives, and looked at the game as part of the challenge in their quest for the ultimate journey. Mr. Bean wished them well, climbed the steps, and leaned on the doorbell.

A small Asian man wearing a white waiter's jacket, black pants, and a bolo tie answered the door. Mr. Bean leaned in close to whisper a few words in the ear of this doorman, who nodded quietly before closing the door. After a few short minutes, a fearsome character, large in build and reeking of garlic, opened the door. The smell was overpowering, but this hulk of a man had the smile of a cat burglar and warmly greeted Mr. Bean. Introductions were made all around, and having passed on the requirements for gaining admission, Mike shook their hands and turned to leave. At the bottom of the walk, he stopped to look as Lefty and Pancho walked inside to chase their dream.

Jimmy "Bag o' Doughnuts" had long held a card game for "friends." He apparently had no last name and no patron had ever summoned up the courage to request it. He essentially ran a full casino, and all manner of propositions could be made on any number of events. He also was the house "muscle" and they knew they would need to keep a close eye on him.

The grand Victorian house sat on top of a hill overlooking downtown Austin. It had several floors with stairways leading up to rooms that weren't mentioned in the brochure. Attractive women in lacy merry widows seemed to act as tour guides to those rooms, and apparently there was a lot to be seen, judging by the amount of time spent inside. The main floor consisted of gaming tables that featured blackjack, roulette, and other games of chance. A lone cigarette girl occasionally paraded around the perimeter of the large room displaying more of her charms than her wares. Her breasts jiggled with every step of her six-inch stilettos and seemed to struggle to escape their captivity. Lefty wore more polyester in one sock than she had on her entire pock-marked body. Her days as a tour guide were long past, but she was kept on staff for her lengthy tongue and keen wit.

Tonight, there were two choices that might hold their attention. A particular basketball wager had caught their eye, but that would be more a game of chance. Lefty knew that no matter how much information he could acquire, it was still up to a handful of other people to decide their fate. A simple flip of a coin would be just as efficient. Wagering on sporting events had not boded well for Lefty in the past, so they declined.

Lefty and Pancho felt that cards had a greater degree of skill involved and relied much less on chance, so without further discussion, they took seats at the bar to survey the situation.

The game tonight was Omaha Hi-Lo. It required a different poker muscle than the other games with which Lefty was more familiar. Omaha was a variation of stud poker where each player received four down cards and there were five community cards that, when combined, were used to make the best or worst hand. The trick was that a player was only able to use two of the four down cards to make that hand. You could split the pot by having the best hand with some-one else having the best low hand, or you could "scoop" them both.

There was an odd assortment of players at the table tonight. It was important to know your opponent in any game of chance, but in no game was it as important as in poker. Looking around, Lefty knew or knew of most of the other players.

The first to get his attention was a portly fellow named DeGlass. He claimed to be a but-ter magnate from Tyler and was partial to small women and large scotches. The Lilliputian women were mostly for his ego, as his rather smallish member became a Louisville Slugger in their elfin hands. He was strangely referred to in certain circles as "*El Jefe de los Jovenes*." This painted an eerie mental image in Lefty's brain, as the translation came out to something like "Boss of the Little Boys." Surrounding yourself with small, young people of both genders did not seem normal on any level, but he looked like an easy mark because any time he had a good hand he would giggle uncontrollably. And besides, he had a huge stack of chips in front of him waiting to be taken away. Lefty eyed him closely as he launched into a single-malt diatribe concerning the butter business about the benefits of using the cream directly from the whole milk as opposed to extracting small amounts of cream from the whey using large centrifuges, or something to that effect. The only reason Lefty listened at all was because whenever DeGlass drank, he affected a strange Cajun patois and assumed the character of a Col. Remy Deauville, complete with a lisp that seemed to amuse the entire table.

Next up was a local character named Alonzo who seemed not to have visited his haberdasher in several years. He wore pricey khakis, button-down cotton shirts, and Bass Weejun loafers that were buffed to a mirror shine, none of which fit him in the least. This smallish black man had a long and storied history around town. He had evidently been a porter at one of the local frat houses and regularly helped himself to clothes that were left lying around after a particularly decadent party. He had disappeared for a time amid rumors that he drank himself to death. The myth was then further exaggerated that he had somehow been stuffed by a friendly alum that dabbled in taxidermy and placed in the secret cellar of said frat house. His reappearance only strengthened his legend. He drank only the clear liquors that contained no "impurities," preferably "gin on with a cherry." "Gin on" apparently meant "gin on the rocks," and by noon he was normally more pickled than Aunt Ellie's okra.

Next to him was a highly disagreeable person who had just finished his second stint in the federal pen. Both sentences were for embezzlement, with a few counts of running a Ponzi scheme thrown in for good measure. He was a self-proclaimed religious zealot, which Lefty thought odd, since he had bilked a large portion of his fellow congregants out of their life savings. He had been caught in his own deadly web of receipts and was tagged by the media with the nickname of "Peter Paul." Lefty deduced this was because he had always robbed Peter to pay Paul. Since getting out of lockup, he had become a degenerate gambler and a prolific liar. This could become a problem for Lefty, as being a prevaricator was the very essence of a good poker player. He, too, would have to be closely watched.

The next player Lefty had never seen before. This was probably due to the fact that he must have been on the fried chicken circuit for a number of years. He was so corpulent that even his ears were obese, and he had the jowls of a fully inflated bullfrog. He was more round than tall, possessed alligator arms, and whistled through his nose when he breathed. He was adorned with a great deal of gold jewelry that jangled whenever he moved, even though the precious metal items appeared to be covered in some sort of body grease. He seemed to play almost every hand, yet still had a considerable wall of jack in front of him.

The only other players of concern were two ex-frat boys who must have thought they were still eighteen. They were actually on the ten-year plan at the university, and were losing money quicker than their fathers could make it. They were dressed exactly the same, wore the same cologne, and had identical haircuts. They reeked of self-importance and an exaggerated sense of entitlement. They fancied themselves poker giants, but tonight must not have been their night. "Biff" and "Skipper" had two nearly empty Jack Daniel's bottles in front of them, which might have been part of the reason for their poor performance. Or perhaps it was just that they were pompous idiots.

Having surveyed their adversaries, Lefty and Pancho once again plotted strategy, hoping all the while that the absinthe would continue to work its magic by freeing their minds and heightening their senses—or at least dulling their sense of dread at losing to this odd assortment of misfits and nincompoops. They stepped out on the back patio to share a smoke and were treated to an Elysian shower of stars racing across the night sky. They took this as a sign of good fortune and made as many wishes on them as possible. Back inside, they ordered two Lone Stars and waited their turn.

It wasn't long before the drunken frat boys were out of money and began to complain that they had been cheated. Throwing around slurred insults, things began to get a little tense. A secret button must have been pushed by the bartender, because Jimmy "Bag o' Doughnuts" appeared through a velvet partition and gave them the heave-ho. They beat a hasty retreat through the front door and out into the night. The barman cleaned up their mess and escorted Lefty to his seat. After he bought in, the game resumed.

Poker can be a game of impossible boredom. Hand after hand can, and should, be thrown away. If a player bluffs at the wrong time, he could be crippled in chips. The key was to be selectively aggressive and patient. Unfortunately, Lefty didn't have the time to wait around for the strongest of hands and was eager to begin play.

Things went back and forth for the better part of an hour. At least he hadn't lost much so far. Pancho paced the bar like a caged panther. Lefty took off the next hand and related to him that he was making the other players nervous. He responded that that was exactly what he had been trying to do. Seeing the beauty of this strategy, Lefty returned to his chair and made up his mind that it was now or never.

It was Alonzo's deal, and he kept muttering something about the great professions of life as he distributed the cards. Something like, "Doctors, lawyers, (mumble, mumble), and submarine operators!" This was actually now making Lefty nervous, and his hands began to shake as he peeked at his cards. Where had this Alonzo character come from? Lefty thought to himself, and just why hadn't *he* been informed of these great professions? It helped that he got next his first good hand of the night, a pair of tens with an ace and a queen, suited. He saw DeGlass raise, then Peter Paul call. Lefty just called the bet and waited for the flop. Another ten came aboard, followed by two over cards. All three checked and the board paired kings on the turn. DeGlass made a large bet, driving out the ex-con. This infuriated Lefty because he had wanted to give this douche bag a real earful and teach him a lesson. Lefty was pretty confident he already had the hand won, but DeGlass was giggling so he only called. The river produced a harmless seven and DeGlass checked. Lefty made a small raise, he was called, and the cards were turned over. His full house left a frown on the once-jolly butter man's face. Definitely a nice pot, with maybe one more to go.

Just then, the curtains parted and a rail-thin man in a red Nudie suit and matching hat entered. He looked straight out of Vegas with all the rhinestones and glitter and easily could have passed as a Porter Wagoner stand-in. Lefty recognized a poker player when he saw one and this was the real McCoy. Luckily, he was making small talk with Jimmy and in no hurry to start play. They strode to the patio and stood in the darkness, the glowing ends of their cigarettes the only clue that they were still there. Peter Paul was dealing this hand and Lefty looked down to see the ace and three of hearts, the five of clubs, and the deuce of spades. Alonzo and DeGlass both called, as did he. Peter Paul folded, again angering Lefty. Two more hearts on the flop and the two men in front of him checked again. This was the time to represent a heart draw and Lefty made a fairly large bet. They both called again and Lefty started to sweat. The four of hearts on the river not only filled his nut flush, but it also gave him a wheel guaranteeing at least a split pot. DeGlass was again giggling, and even Alonzo had become aware of this. He folded and DeGlass made a large raise. Lefty thought for a moment and pushed all of his chips into the pot. This caused DeGlass to pause. He checked his hand again and saw that his flush was still there. He called. Lefty turned over his hand and leaned back in his chair, owning the only flush that could beat DeGlass's. He was able to scoop the entire pot when the portly gent had only an eight high for the low part of the wager. The oleo magnate was enraged and knocked over his large scotch. The secret button was again pushed and Jimmy reappeared quickly. This time he didn't scowl, though. In fact, he looked a bit taken aback. Lefty wasn't ready for that and slowly looked over his shoulder. There, perched on his bar stool like a falcon, Pancho was cleaning his nails with the Bowie knife. He never even looked up as Jimmy slowly approached Lefty and mentioned that it might be best if they left, considering that weapons were a definite no-no at this game. Since that was their intention the whole time, the two friends silently walked to the cashier, then to the front door and down the steps. As they made their way down the hill, both let out a huge sigh of relief, followed by bursts of laughter. God and karma had certainly been on their side this night, and they returned to the Continental Club on angel wings.

After repaying their stake to Wyn, Pancho wisely decided it was time to hail a cab. Even with the capitol building straight ahead of them and all the security that that entailed, it would be prudent not to walk the streets with this large of a sum of money at one in the morning. The cabby was a friend of Townes's and knew of a quick route back to the house, but the boys wanted to take a more scenic one. The cabdriver was fine with that, as he had needed a fare for over an hour. The two grilled him with questions about his livelihood, his favorite customers, the drunks and the hookers. Their eyes were wide as saucers from the tales he told by the time he pulled up in front of the house. Exiting the cab, they heard, "Whoopee!" as Townes bounded off his porch, ran across the lawn, and jumped in the front seat of the cab. Lefty knew that Townes had been up for a few days, and if it wasn't for the fact that they probably wouldn't return before dawn, the two thought about climbing back in and joining the party. Remembering the gangster roll in his boot, however, Lefty said good-bye and watched the taillights disappear into the mist. Onward through the fog, indeed...

After climbing the steps, they were happy to see that some ice remained in the Villa Capri bucket. Pancho was appointed bartender and Lefty retreated to his library to stash their cash. He moved an upholstered chair and pulled up the loose board in the hardwood floor. There, he deposited the currency among other treasures kept there—a few baseball cards, a misappropriated ashtray from the Ritz in Paris, a garter whose original owner had long ago been forgotten, and several Mexican coins that had been collected on the many trips to Matamoros and Tijuana. He replaced the board, returned the chair, and made his way to the porch.

He found Pancho in a wistful mood as he offered Lefty some of the green spirit. For these many years, Pancho had stayed single, worked, and enjoyed life while he lived in Houston on the top floor of a luxurious high-rise building called The Eleganza. It *was* elegant, yet it had none of the charm of a clapboard house with a wraparound porch and a yard full of oak trees in suburban Austin.

"Left, I have always thought that you have everything I don't...a loving woman, some animals and a garden to tend to, a fine house with character, that kind of thing. I just go to work, come home at night, rattle a few cages every now and then...and fuck everything with a pulse that I can get my hands on, mind you...but something's missing. Maybe it's because I never had all those kids in my family like you did...or not. Shit, it must be the Fairy talking. I mean, really, all I have to look forward to is our big rendezvous every spring. It's the highlight of my year. Don't get me wrong, I'm happy almost *all* of the time and I never go wanting for anything. You're just lucky, I guess. They should have called you Lucky instead of Lefty. I wonder what is going to happen tomorrow..." Pancho trailed off and followed it with a slow, very large grin.

Perhaps tomorrow would change a few things for them both. Lefty marveled that soon he would fulfill his lifelong dream. He would literally and figuratively get on the bus the next day and finally, after all these years, run away and join the circus—of freaks.

CHAPTER
THIRTEEN

God opened his heavenly eyes the next morning at the normal time. This in turn caused the occupants of the house to stir and make their way downstairs. The espresso had already brewed and was waiting for them. Dixie was to chair an important meeting today and had risen quite early. There were two yellow roses lying on the table anticipating their arrival and Lefty placed them in a tall, thin bud vase. Neither of the friends spoke for several minutes. They were both quite solemn as the day began, but Lefty knew how to change that. He walked to the library and found the needed tonic. He placed the worn platter on the turntable, cued the needle and waited. After a scratchy moment or two, the Allman Brothers' "One Way Out" from the album *At Fillmore East* leaped out of the speakers and shook them by the ears. *Laissez les bons temps rouler, mon frere.* Indeed, let the good times roll, my brother.

After a quick breakfast of fruit and melon, they grabbed the backpack and headed out the door, carefully stepping over the two comatose, and apparently deaf, cats that lay in their path. Lefty had appointed Cal as his chargé d'affaires to look in on Dixie and the kids during his absence, and as the pair closed the door behind them, Lefty felt confident in his choice. Looking across the street, they saw Cal and Townes reclining in the rattan papasan chairs that lined Townes's porch. The two men immediately jumped to attention. Lefty and Pancho saluted as their friends fired only a two-gun salute that was, thankfully, aimed over their heads. His neighbor, Carol, appeared in her doorway wearing some lime green high-tops and little else, looking for what had caused all the ruckus. Finding nothing to further her ire, she turned and mooned the neighborhood. Lefty looked to the skies in gratitude that the weaponry their friends had used for this sign of respect today was only harmless pellet guns, since her perfectly shaped backside made an inviting target. After a quick wave, Lefty and Pancho hurried to chase their fate.

Barton Springs was quiet this time of the morning. It had been a meeting place for the Indian tribes that inhabited Texas for thousands of years. It was the fourth-largest spring in the state and stayed at a constant sixty-eight degrees year-round. After changing into their Birdwells Beach Britches in the men's locker room, they chose a spot (fittingly) on the left bank and laid down two large towels. Pancho opened the backpack, found the cigar box, and retrieved the precious blue bandana. He ceremoniously unfolded the material and took out the contents. The buttons had been prepared the night before using the Henckels paring knife. The tufts of hair found on the top of the buttons reportedly contained strychnine, and to avoid the queasiness that came with the ingestion of this poison, they were cautiously cored out. Lefty's road man had said this was hogwash, but they would rather be safe than sorry. What he did not tell them about was the peculiarly nauseating odor that was emitted by the buttons once they were cut. This alone was enough to cause the involuntary gagging that had plagued Lefty for so many years. They looked at each other and began to chew, each keeping down several pieces of the rubbery cacti. They had planned on Cal joining in this journey so there was more than enough for the two friends. After they took Cal's portion, Lefty and Pancho tried to act like they knew what they were doing. Remembering some pictures of an actual Indian ceremony, they sat cross-legged facing each other and tried to do some sort of meditation, praying for guidance and leadership. This became comical after awhile. They gave up entirely when two buxom ladies made silly faces at them when they strode by, and Pancho began to fart. The queasiness had given way to the hilarity of passing malodorous gas, and Pancho simply stated, "My farts have always smelled like ice cream. I don't know why that is or what kind of ice cream it is that they smell like, but they just do. What do yours smell like?"

Ignoring this blather, Lefty lay back on the cool, damp grass and waited for the flatulence to subside. After what seemed like hours, Pancho grumbled, "Goddamn it. I don't feel one mother-fucking thing. I think we was robbed. Not by Annie, and tell her I said so, but that douche bag that sold them to *her* was a complete dickweed and he might want to start keeping his will up-to-date. All dressed up and no place to go. *Gawd-damn it.*"

Lefty hadn't felt a thing, either, but something told him that things *were* a little different now. After another forty-five minutes, they angrily shrugged it off as a "misappropriation of funds" and decided to take a swim. In unison, they rose, walked to the edge of the cement bank to the left of the lifeguard stand, looked at one another for a moment with eyes as large as saucers, and dove into the mystic...

CHAPTER
FOURTEEN

The Conch Republic

Lefty opened his eyes around Mile Marker 20. Swirls of haze drifted before him and it felt as if his entire body was numb. As he became more aware of his surroundings and tried to straighten in his seat, the bus hit a pothole and threw his face into the tattered seat cushion in front of him. His head began to throb and his ears were filled with what sounded alternately like foghorns and European police sirens. He pretended nothing was wrong, but it was clear that he was dazed. From what, he did not know, but the sounds in his head should have given him a clear clue that something was just not right. Rubbing his hands together, he found his palms were sweaty, almost clammy. He wiped them on his jeans and looked around for Pancho. "Where is that son of a bitch," Lefty said to himself. "Of all the times to go running off..."

His third eye had been functional the entire trip and it had seen the bayous of Louisiana; the cotton fields of Alabama, filled with the sweet harmony of old Negro spirituals; the coast of Mississippi, with the ancient shrimp boats that had been passed down from generation to generation, across the panhandle of Florida, and the final swoop straight down the state, crossing the Everglades and into the mouth of the Keys. They had passed Key Largo, Islamorada, with its famous Tiki Bar, through Marathon, and were now closing in on their destination. Since having boarded the "Eden Express" sometime yesterday, they had traveled nonstop almost fifteen hundred miles. Their fellow passengers had spent the time passing around cheap wine and questionable cigarettes. Somewhere around Pascagoula, Pancho had joined in the merriment. He had always had a superior constitution and could survive at peak levels with little or no sleep. He soon noticed that Lefty had awakened, and flew back down the aisle and crashed into his seat noisily with unbridled energy. Before the clamor had subsided, he was already explaining, or trying to explain, a strange vision he had had concerning a disabled girl of great beauty he would soon meet.

"Left! Thank God you're awake. You wouldn't *believe* the things that were going on in this damn bus while you were in the Land of Nod," Pancho loudly whispered, causing several heads to turn to see what was up.

Lefty rubbed the sleep from his eyes and put his third one, or the "mind's eye," to bed. "What in the hell are you talking about? I've been here the whole time...haven't I?" Lefty said, still shaking cobwebs from his brain.

"Well, you were and you weren't. Unlike you, dipstick, I have met every single person on this bus, and I swear to Christ, there's not a sane one in the bunch. I tell you, they're our kind of people. That crazy one sitting up there in front, close to the driver and passing him joints, he thinks he's an alien! I shit you not. Don't even go near him. I told him you had scabies and needed to be quarantined and I think he bought it. He's been eyeing you ever since."

Lefty leaned over Pancho and stuck his head out into the aisle. Sure enough, there was a character in an outlandish get-up staring back at him.

"But wait," Pancho kept on, "that's not the best part. I had an out-of-body thing going on there for awhile, and I saw that I—well, we—would meet this fine-looking gal with some kind of wings on her back. Just like you with Dixie back there in Port Aransas! I swear, she was fine as frog's fur and had a rack that kept her falling forward all the time. She looked just like Easter Sunday, blonde hair full of flowers, tall, did I mention her tits? There was this one little nagging thing, though...she seemed to be deformed somehow. I think she was missing an arm or something. Nothing I couldn't handle, you see. I mean, I've let worse-looking girls give my crank a yank, if you know what I mean. Holy crap, just so fine, though.

And those titties..." He settled back into his seat and let out a low sigh. And then he farted.

As the entire busload of people watched the last miles of this two-lane blacktop count down, Lefty noticed a sign outside on a run-down bar that read: "Free Beer Tomorrow." The irony never dawned on him, and he made a mental note of this giveaway, vowing to return. Anticipation was beginning to fill the coach, and as the group passed Mile Marker 1, a great roar filled the air and swirled around the stale compartment. This signpost also signaled the appearance of the rusted and burned-out cars, school buses, and other assorted vehicles that lined the road leading them into the Conch Republic.

The path into Key West was a parking lot heaven for these old and well-used vehicles. Some pointed the way into town and had been abandoned when the last gasp of gas had failed to reach their carburetors. They had literally come to the end of the highway and fallen a mile or less short of their destination. Footprints marked the sides of the highway where happy, sandaled travelers had trekked the last bit of the journey, carrying their belongings on their backs. The footprints leading away from the city belonged to travelers whose vehicles had met a more violent demise. Charred skeletons of steel were left angry and on fire when they became impotent and provided no means of escape from the lunatic fringe. Some still smoldered and smelled of burnt rubber.

The coach pulled into the sleepy depot, and with a loud *whoosh* of steam and screech of the brakes, they came to a stop. The passengers departed into the dream world that was Key West. They gathered their belongings, meager as they were, secured a locker at the bus terminal, and set out anxiously to explore the island.

Even at this early hour, the streets had people going on about their business before the craziness of a normal day in paradise set in. Bicycles and old scooters seemed to be the transportation of choice since parking spaces were a rare commodity. Lefty and Pancho decided to hoof it and made their way to a local taco stand, where there was a line of four or five people waiting for their orders. These were obviously locals, and locals knew where to find great food. They were all smiling broadly and seemed to be saying, "Yes, we're glad you were able to make it. We're your friends here and all are welcome. Make yourselves at home and feel free to just be alive."

They gratefully received their tacos and grabbed a city map from a rack on the side of the rickety stand before finding a bench where they nibbled on the snacks, knowing the next wave of euphoria could wash over them at any moment. Peyote, like other hallucinogens, ebbed and flowed like the ocean, never the same way twice and never as expected. They knew the waves were coming for sure, though. Expectation of coming events was one thing. But the anticipation of the event and its unfamiliar timetable made them tingle with uneasiness. Unfortunately, the food did not sit well with this tingly feeling, and they quickly disposed of the tacos nearby.

They didn't have long to wait. Soon, their synapses were welded together and this brave new world of Key West opened up to them. Sighs of contentment, fear, harmony, anxiety, and joy would be the only verbal communication they would have for the next several hours, as the corners of their mouths turned up in perpetual grins and their pupils once again grew to a comical size.

With great difficulty, they scanned the map making mental notes of essential places they must visit. Lefty tried to refold the map to put it in his pocket. Unfortunately, the map wasn't cooperating, and he tried once again only with worse results. Such a simple act had become an unwelcome chore, and finally he crushed the map into a ball and tossed it into the hungry receptacle on top of the uneaten repast. This was disturbing to Lefty, as he had always considered himself an expert in the art of map folding. His mind switched gears as he saw Pancho disappear around a corner. Lefty looked toward the sky and silently laughed at Pancho's favorite line, "If you're waiting on me, you got your hat on backward." If there was ever a time for Pancho to pull that quip out and use it, this certainly was it. He scurried down the street and caught up with Pancho as he turned onto Duval Street, and a whole new vista came into view.

Duval is world-famous and rightly so. Things that would be considered inappropriate behavior in any other city in the country, with the possible exception of New Orleans, were everyday occurrences here. The public nudity, from partial up to and including full-frontal, was common. Life on any island was usually very laid-back and casual, but this was approaching the absurd. Pancho was intrigued and led the pair to a prime viewing spot. If midday was like this, what would the evening bring? With lecherous grins on their faces, they surveyed this parade of life.

Besides the barely clothed people, a squadron of creepy antique dolls with lifelike eyes that opened and shut on cue paraded before them wearing little brown uniforms. Each of them had a plastic baby bottle in her right hand and saluted the two in unison as they passed. Pancho and Lefty clapped again like the old wind-up monkeys in time to the marching, with broad smiles. This was highly entertaining. But out of the corner of Lefty's eye, on the roof of the building across the street, he spied a curious sight. There, above the sign that read:

R. C. Moriarity, Accountant
Author of the best-selling book
"Tax Evasion Made Easy"

was a character that seemed to be waving a black flag in lazy figure eights across the blue sky. Was this some kind of warning? For a moment, Lefty thought he heard his name being called, but that would have been impossible. He nudged Pancho and pointed toward the figure with his chin. Pancho squinted to get a better look and cocked his head to hear above the clamor of the parading dolls. Hearing nothing but the clatter of the tiny plastic doll shoes as they moved by the friends, Pancho turned to see a patrolman approaching them. This was Monroe County Deputy Mort Snerd. His rayon trousers glistened in the bright sunlight and emitted sparks when his thighs rubbed together as he walked. Having just stepped off the bus here in heaven, Lefty and Pancho were in no mood to be placed in shackles and thrown underneath the jailhouse just for enjoying the sights. Not wanting to draw unwanted attention, Pancho screamed "Fire!" and pointed down the sandy avenue. This apparently worked, because Snerd rushed off to the beauty parlor to find the fire marshal, who was having his hair and nails done. Proud of their dodge, the two Texans returned to the amusement happening on the street. Occasionally, Lefty would return his gaze to the rooftop to see if the flag waver had returned, but eventually gave up. After a time, they found it hard to concentrate on just one thing, even something as riveting and compelling as this spectacle had become, and with a finger pointing the way, Pancho led Lefty forward with a new mission in mind.

CHAPTER
FIFTEEN

They found their way to 400 Front Street and entered the hallowed doors. What the Butler Cabin in Augusta is to golf, the Hog's Breath Saloon is to the world of hedonism. Bikers in general, and their subspecies, the "one percenters," were always ending a poker run there and it had become part of the debauched landscape. With Outlaws, Bandidos, and even a few stray Hells Angels making the pilgrimage to this mecca, one might think there would be lots of skirmishes and brawling occurring around here, but that was just not the case. Occasionally, yes, but no more than with the idiot tourists after a snoot full of rum runners.

As they entered, they were relieved to find the place rather quiet, unusual even for this time of day. As normal, they found a seat in the corner and tried to stop gritting their teeth. They could have chosen to sit outside on the deck, but the soothing darkness had, at least for the moment, stopped the kaleidoscope of tropical colors assaulting their eyelids. Because they were still without the ability to communicate with the outside world, they were happy to see that menus had been left on the table next to them. Quickly snatching them, they settled down to pretend that they were able to read them. As Lefty looked at each word, it would melt away and drip off the page. He found this totally engrossing. He held a napkin below the menu but was not able to catch the drippings. The words seemed to evaporate as soon as they left the page. He closed his eyes and stabbed a finger at the bill of fare. The item on which his finger had landed seemed to be held there as if by magic. Words around it melted away, but his finger had a hold on this one. Unfortunately, a banana daiquiri did not seem appealing at this juncture. He followed this procedure several more times and finally found what he was looking for—tequila. Pancho noticed this little game and tried it for himself. Amazed that this was the solution, they seemed to relax a bit. The only problem was that you had to keep your finger in place or your selection might once again be lost in the ether.

Soon, a waitress approached their table and began her spiel about the chef's specials. Food wasn't on their minds. Libations were. Pancho pointed to a rum runner with a floater of 151, while Lefty chose the key lime margarita with double hooch. She retreated with a puzzled look on her face. She began to talk very animatedly with Carlson the bartender, and then slunk away with a frown. She must be new to the job, for this saloon had certainly seen far stranger occurrences over the years. The two shrugged their shoulders and let their minds wander.

Just as Lefty was beginning to solve the mysteries of life, the waitress arrived with their drinks. "I hope I got this right, fellas. I've waited tables before but never in a place like this. So many things I ain't ever heard of before. One guy just last week asked me for some 'sex on the beach' and I just thought I'd die! He thought I must have been stupid or something. He had a lot of nerve asking me for that. It was early in the day, too! Anything happens again like that I might just be on my way. Okay, I've got the rum one for you and the tequila one for Mister Bashful," she said, as she carefully placed the barrel-like glasses in front of them. "I hear you guys aren't much for talking, and I just wanted you to know that my aunt had an ailment just like yours. We always used to ask her, 'Cat got your tongue?'" The two friends erupted in laughter, which scared her immeasurably. Embarrassed, she left the table, threw her apron on the bar and walked out the front door, never to return. The bartender winked in their direction, chuckled to himself, and went back to his newspaper.

The two enjoyed their cocktails while Lefty tried to remember what he had been thinking about in the moments just before the unexpected early retirement of the hired help. Unfortunately, his mind wandered aimlessly about, trying to center on one thought, but he was soon on to other theorems and postulates that flew into his head. He was headed to another breakthrough just when there was a cacophonous crash. A waiter with a crowded tray of drinks dropped it all at their feet on his way to the deck. With frayed nerves, Lefty wondered if he should go check his shorts. Unchecked and uncontrolled body spasms could quickly put a heavy damper on their day. He sped to the bathroom in a panic, but just as quickly returned with a smile of relief—the tragedy had been narrowly averted.

He sat down and glanced toward the front door. A line of people had formed in front of a small window just inside the main entrance, where they exchanged what appeared to be currency for some sort of merchandise. The line grew as time passed. People from all walks of life had found their way to this small window and were content to wait in line to be the next chosen one.

After a while, the bar became almost full. It was time for a change of scenery, so Lefty motioned for another round, this time in to-go cups. When the barkeep presented the drinks and bill, Lefty lifted his arm and pointed to the people in line with a gnarled, scaly finger and a confused look on his face. Carlson glanced over his shoulder and laughed. He said that the Hog's shirt sales had eclipsed the restaurant's receipts for food and beverage. It seemed as if everybody could not live without a sweatshirt, T-shirt, or bandana. This should have come as no surprise to Lefty. As he had traveled the world, he had seen the shirts everywhere. From east to west, and north to south, he had seen them in abundance. It reminded him of another restaurant that seemed to have the same good fortune. There was a smallish café across from Buckingham Palace in London that was a haven for expatriates from the states. One could get a decent hamburger and a cold Budweiser in the land of inedible food, all the while looking at some pretty impressive rock-and-roll memorabilia from around the world. The only problem was that to get a shirt one had to travel to Europe. Lefty mused that perhaps one day he would try and make it over to see what all the commotion was about. Lefty ignored the gnarled, scaly appearance of his fingers and licked them with his now very-dry serpentine tongue.

They left an outrageous tip, knowing they needed to make and keep as many friends as possible. They passed the crowded window outside the door and found a bench in the shade. As luck would have it, the Conch Republic Train was turning the corner and pulled up in front of them. This trolley was free to all and they bounded aboard. This was an ideal way to traverse the city and see the sights, all from the relative comfort of the slow-moving train. The engineer was resplendent in his cap and overalls. At his feet sat an old oil can with a long, thin spout that reminded Lefty of the wading birds he had seen as they arrived in town. The two leaned back and let the aroma of the island's jasmine and gardenias fill their nostrils. This bouquet of ambrosia swirled round their nasal cavities, straight to the brain and down to their toes.

Pancho gazed down to look at the tracks and was surprised to see that there were none. He glanced at Lefty and back to the non-tracks, and grinned. "Ain't life grand!" he seemed to mouth. "We're riding a magical train in a magical city!" As they chugged along, they were amazed to behold sights that boggled their minds. Chickens and six-toed cats filled the streets and trees. Birds with hideous beaks and unimaginably colorful plumage filled the skies. They seemed to leave pastel vapor trails as they dove and gracefully climbed back to the heavens. They made their flight amid the hundreds of rainbows that littered the landscape, darting in and out through the psychedelic arcs. The sky appeared yellow and the sun was blue. Up was down and black was white. Angry chickens chased the train, brandishing their disturbing and repellent talons. The two friends recoiled in horror as razor-sharp beaks nipped at their heels. Things were now taking a decidedly ugly turn. Eventually, the engineer must have thrown more coal in the firebox because the trolley left the angry poultry behind.

Glad to be rid of this surreal encumbrance, they once again turned their attention to the chromosomally challenged cats. Unlike the crazed fowl, these felines were the picture of beauty and grace. They lazed on the walls that bordered most of the houses along the street. Many were also in the trees catching a midday snooze. Others sat like sphinxes and watched the insanity that was Key West parade by in front of them.

At one time, Pancho had been the proud owner of a six-toed cat, so he wasn't overly impressed at the first glimpses of these beauties. He became more concerned when they had traveled more than a mile and not seen a single normal cat. By the time they arrived at the Hemingway House, with a virtual flock of the six-toed variety wandering about, he about lost it. They had basically overrun the property with their mutant paws and ringed tails. Lefty amused himself by pondering about the size of the cat box that would be needed to service this herd of animals.

Meanwhile, the train had stopped in front of Hemingway's home for a few minutes. Most of the passengers departed. The boys were afraid to leave their seats at this point. In fact, it was impossible to move their feet at all for some reason. Lefty noticed the intricate details of the architecture that surrounded the home of his childhood hero. Perhaps another time they might enter this hallowed sanctuary. Lefty remembered with great clarity that Ernest was nothing if not a creature of habit, too, who would rise early in the morning and write for several hours. Afternoons were for drinking and fishing with friends. Pre-Castro Cuba was a favorite haunt, as was Sloppy Joe's back on the island, where he always commandeered the same bar stool. *Mojitos* were his drink of choice and barkeeps across the island had been taught the secret recipe. Lefty had never heard of one outside of the Keys, but if they were that good, well, maybe one day they would catch on.

His dreams of catching giant marlin and brawling alongside his bearded hero came to an abrupt end when the train lurched forward and they resumed their trek. They passed Truman's Little White House and the home where Tennessee Williams wrote first drafts of *Cat on a Hot Tin Roof* and others. Victorian houses were everywhere, painted in all colors tropical, with the bright blues, Bermuda pinks, and canary yellows being the most prolific and abundant. As they turned back down Duval, a wave of energetic fervor washed over them and they decided to make a move. Unfortunately, they didn't relay this to the conductor and, forgetting that the laws of gravity were still in effect, tumbled out at a crowded corner where they fell in a heap at the feet of an appreciative crowd. Sudden moves were worrisome in their present state of mind and needed to be avoided. Embarrassed, they shook off as much of the street dust as possible, checked for any sign of blood and hurried away. It was time to fall back and regroup, if only for a little while. If they only knew what lay ahead for them...

They found a side street off of Duval and with some difficulty scaled the low wall. Trying to get as comfortable as possible, they realized they had a splendid view of the goings-on down along the main drag. Life, in all its abhorrent and beautiful forms, was unfolding right in front of them. And there were no chickens to be seen.

C H A P T E R
S I X T E E N

The heartland was certainly not ready for this Daliesque cast of characters bouncing around before them in the sticky tropical sun. Beefy men from the Corn Belt would snatch up their bosomy wives and wonderfully average offspring, locking them in the root cellar, until this scourge of freethinkers and castaways had passed by, should this tribe ever decide to pull up stakes and venture away from paradise to parade down Main Street, USA. There was a reason this plague chose to live on the literal fringe of society, and it was clearly that they were not welcome in your hometown. This seemed to work very well for everyone involved, as *they* did not want to be in *your* hometown in the first place. They chose to stay away from *you*, not the other way around, and it made for a delicious scenario to observe *you* cross over the borders of taste and dignity to venerate at *their* altar for a day or two before escaping the craziness and returning to the comfort of idyllic lives of pot roasts and marital infidelity. The denizens of Key West had most certainly taken up the sage road man's advice and become gloriously contrary to ordinary. The simultaneous look between the two friends signaled an agreement of thoughts and the visions continued.

The inhabitants of the tropical burg were a cross-pollination of all human genres. Several species were more prominent than others. First, there were the artists—painters, sculptors, fine craftsmen, and body painters. Novelists, actors, would-be poet laureates, movie directors, and others of their ilk filled the bars, street corners, and storefronts, hawking their talents to anyone who would listen. Early in the morning, writers would hunch over crumpled notebooks hashing out the next great American novel while nursing a warm beer. Actors would practice their craft with street soliloquies to no one in particular. Visitors would find this incredibly interesting, invariably heckling them during the "performance," while the locals barely acknowledged their existence.

Another species were the street performers. There were jugglers, fire-eaters, harlequins, dwarves and midgets, contortionists, balloon artists, comics, unicyclists, psychics, musicians of every genre, pirates, escape artists, and magicians. They were everywhere, but mostly in Old Town.

Then there were the blasphemers, pagans, infidels, and idolaters. They would burn effigies at regular intervals if the chosen subject didn't specifically agree with their dogma, and typical targets included any American president, past or present, the church, and the upper class. They would spout their militaristic gibberish on the street to anyone who would listen, which, invariably, was nobody.

The gays had gained a strong foothold on the island and weren't about to let loose their grip. The streets were filled with leather boys and their fey devotees. Truck-driving lesbians and their lipstick counterparts traded makeup secrets with the overflow of transvestites and transsexuals. A whole bar scene was devoted to their class and they filled the boites to the rafters nightly. Some of the most outrageous parades the island had ever witnessed consisted of nearly naked boys in slingshot bikinis and hairy men in drag. Tolerance of sexual orientation here would be a harbinger of things to come.

Any fishing town worth its salt will always have its fair share of captains, mates, and deckhands. The Keys were unusual in that, by sheer luck, they were located in the sport fishing capital of the universe, where many world-class fishing tournaments were held every year. It would be perfectly natural to assume that, in this industry, one could make a decent living. Unfortunately, any winnings or charter fees would quite possibly be gone the next morning, as captains especially were known for buying half the town free drinks all night after a big win. As a result, they were often forced to buy large bags of beans and rice to get them through the slow months. The winning captain was usually given a gold Rolex watch by the men who actually took home the big money and there would be no parting with that trophy under any circumstances. So, in the off-season, you might easily catch a glimpse of a raggedy captain wearing worn-out Top-Siders, a tattered long-sleeved shirt, crusty shorts, and a faded cap, and sporting a fifteen-thousand-dollar watch on each arm going through trash cans looking for half-eaten hamburgers.

The last order was the down-and-outers. They knew that escape was entirely possible, if push came to shove, for they were at the southern-most point of the continental United States and only ninety miles from Cuba. It was the perfect jumping-off point if you had people that were looking for you, and, for a price, all manner of boats were available for hire. There were drug dealers and smugglers, strippers and hookers, thieves and con artists, the homeless who flocked here for the temperate weather, modern-day pirates, burned-out hippies who found California too cold, treasure hunters, and, of course, ex-cons. Tattoo artists should not be mentioned in this class, for they made a decent, if not a great, living. Finding a bride in the Keys was problematic if you followed the dictum of "more teeth than tattoos." Any true Conch was the proud owner of at least one visible tattoo and one other that might be revealed in more intimate moments—like strolling down Duval Street.

And then there were the tourists. Virtually any local that lived on an island, in a seaside village or resort destination, relied on them to make a living. Unfortunately, that did not mean that they weren't despised. A strange sense of entitlement made them think they were superior to those visitors that stepped off the cruise ships or made the long journey down U.S. 1 to spend their money. Like clockwork, every hour or so another ship would tie up, lower the gangway, and let the garish hordes descend upon paradise. There seemed to be a sort of unwritten dress code for these excursionists. Ill-fitting and brightly colored Bermuda shorts, terry-cloth tops, black socks, and white loafers were the norm, with the occasional New Yorker dripping in gold and some breed of polyester blend not meant for tropical climes. Almost all of them carried some class of camera, eager to take home memories of the debauchery that they had encountered to show their buddies around the water cooler or at their suburban supper clubs as proof that, "Yup, by Gawd, that is a naked tit."

Pancho and Lefty seemed to be in their own little world of bliss just watching the partici-pants of this parade of humanity. The constant movement on the street was like the peyote trip itself: never the same twice, always in flux and infinitely interesting. Lefty's head swirled with sen-sory overload. It seemed to be akin to one giant, throbbing amoeba crammed inside his skull, and even if he had wanted to, there was nothing he could do about it. There seemed to have been a cleansing of the windows to his soul. The strips of gauze that had enveloped his head since he was a child were slowly being unwrapped like the layers of an onion. His ocular deficiencies were now a thing of the past and his world was clear, crisp, and sharp. His intellectual perception had become so acute that he found himself solving complicated algebraic equations that had haunted him since high school. He pulled out the diary to take notes on this breakthrough and almost fell off his perch. Regaining his balance, he began to scribble furiously. Proud of himself, he rejoined the drama playing itself out on the street.

Without warning, things changed in a flash. As another explosive wave crashed over them, Pancho began to weep and, through his tears, blurted out, "I've missed you, Lefty." This was troubling to Lefty on many fronts. First of all, he had never seen his pal cry before, and although he was sure that it had happened at some time or another, Lefty had never been there to witness it. Second, as far as he could remember, they had occupied this wall for what seemed like hours, close enough to touch each other with little or no effort. Not knowing what to say, Lefty tried to comfort his friend and wrapped an arm around his broad shoulders; that provided the needed psychic spark of understanding between the two. While Lefty was admiring this parade of hedonistic acolytes, Pancho had left and ventured abroad, his mind breaking free of his body and into another world. He had climbed Alpine glaciers, sipped café au lait in Parisian cafes, walked the streets of dusty Jakarta, and drunk Pernod in the bars of Lisbon. All of this, alone and naked. He had returned frayed and afraid. Not sure whether to be happy for him or concerned, Lefty recovered his tongue and spoke in calming tones until this wave of ecstasy passed and rolled back to the sea.

"Pancho, hey, it's me. Everything's gonna be alright. I'm here and you were just...just...out there for a bit. I'm not gonna leave you here and you aren't gonna leave me. Just remember to stick with the plan. Ride it out." Lefty looked away slowly and murmured to himself, "Shit, I wonder if that is gonna happen to me soon. I think this ride has only just begun."

Their brains had become a nest of angry hornets and the street was too hot for snakes. Vises crushed their virgin skulls and brutal, parapsychological images roamed the countryside looking for safety amid the confusion. Uncircumcised men of the cloth threw pointed daggers at themselves and bathed in filth while sinister necromancers leaned in darkened doorways calling out for morbid pleasures of the flesh. Preternatural voices sang dirges to unknown corpses while thundering tribal beats and the howls of unseen jungle beasts rose and fell, filling the auditory landscape. Where was all the fucking screaming coming from? A large cross-eyed cat glared at them in a strange manner with its ears pinned back threateningly. Confused, but not wanting to lose this opportunity of retreat, they regrouped, carefully slid down the wall, and made their way to the epicenter and headquarters of all things Key West.

Sloppy Joe's had made its debut in 1933 and moved to its present location in 1937. The Key West landmark was a grand bar with a storied history. It seemed never to close, but actually it did, from four a.m. to nine a.m. In earlier days it would close for a "siesta hour" in the afternoons, allowing patrons time to recharge for the evening bacchanalia. This was a perfect time for the two to slip in and quiet their nerves with some high-octane refreshment. It perfectly fit their needs for the moment, as it was dark, friendly, and quiet at this time of day. As their eyes adjusted to the dim surroundings, they spotted a prime viewing area for both the bar and the street. Double margaritas, straight up with extra salt, were just what the doctor ordered, as did the guys. The drinks arrived, and before the waitress even left the table, another round was marshaled. She returned to find the two glasses bone-dry. Pancho's unusually large tongue was removing the excess salt from his lips when she managed to ask casually, "You able to do any other tricks with that snake?"

She now had Pancho's *full* attention. "Yes, and I just might have to teach you one or two." he said, flicking his erect taster at her. "And just when do you get off, young lady?"

She laughed as she turned and said playfully, "I get off *every* time, sugah." She danced away and Pancho made a mental note to return at closing time.

As the tequila warmed their bellies and calmed their brains, they sat back in their chairs and took in this famous locale. The ceiling was a mélange of lingerie, mostly bras, and business cards that had been collected over the years and were now nicotine-stained and weathered. This brought up a curious imagery of low morals and bad behavior that somehow the guys had missed out on. Perhaps tonight they might be privy to such an event.

Near the door, a local troubadour nicknamed Scamp was setting up his sound system and microphone. He wore his Conch uniform proudly and was already on his second beer. The uniform consisted of flip-flops, board shorts, a flowered shirt, and a hat woven from palm fronds. Beards and moustaches were not required, but those and long stringy hair were prevalent. Being so near the door, he acted as an accidental shill, even though one was not needed in this place of honor. He started off with some island covers before moving on to his original material. The two friends decided he was pretty good and ordered another round. A new waitress approached their table and Pancho realized he had missed his chance with the other. He let it go and noisily slurped his refreshment.

Their thoughts were suddenly interrupted by the sounds of a jalopy moving down the road at a very high rate of speed. Sparks flew out of the tailpipe like fireworks while Dean manned the wheel with his head out the window searching for his drunken father, and Sal looked around madly for familiar signposts leading to the Mexican border. They sped off in a cloud of smelly fumes and lingering dust. Soon, the townspeople went about their sleepy business of looking for somewhere to go.

In the middle of this comfortable setting, something caught Lefty's third eye. Without moving his head, the eye followed a path to the far corner where he saw Catherine of Aragon crumbing her royal table. She properly folded her lace napkin, rose, and ceded her seat to Anne Boleyn, who took her Tudor chair. Lefty's suspicious eye blinked and she was gone.

As the afternoon shadows began to grow longer, the two became restless and needed a new plan of attack. Food was out of the question, since their stomachs still churned and roiled, though not in an unpleasant manner. Lefty glanced out the front window and saw people herding like sheep, all in one direction, moving back to Duval Street and turning toward the town square. What an interesting turn of events. The bill was quickly paid and they joined the crowd.

Everyone held large cups of some powerful concoction or another. They moved as one, and Lefty decided that they, too, would become part of the "sheeple nation"—the "more" blind following the "just" blind. Lemmings to the sea, as it were. As the group neared Mallory Square, they were joined by other flocks from different parts of town. The horde made its grand entrance into a large open area that was indeed a circus. There were tightrope walkers, sword swallowers, fire-eaters, trained animals, and dancers. Around the periphery, stalls were set up where you could buy anything you desired, from cold beverages, food, and alcohol to hats, shirts, and souvenirs. This evidently was a nightly party, and even locals who had not become too jaded made it as often as possible to see the brilliant sunsets. Mellowed by the sweet juice of the agave, the boys tootled around and watched the festivities. Everything was going well until Pancho saw the clown.

He recoiled in fear and backed slowly away from the approaching menace. This coulraphobia, the fear of clowns, had begun when, as a child, his father had taken him to his first big-top experience. He had, in his mind, been assaulted by a monster with large hands, feet, and nose. He was unable to sleep for weeks, and still to this day checked under his bed before closing his eyes for the night. Luckily, Bozo had other victims in mind and wandered harmlessly away. Unnerved, Pancho began looking over his shoulder every few steps until he was sure "it" had left the vicinity. Thank heavens it was a large square.

The setting sun picked up speed as it neared the horizon and the excitement among the flock grew to a frenzied crescendo. Another wave seemed to hit the pair as the golden orb drowned in the ocean and disappeared. The crowd roared with appreciation and continued the festivities. The boys knew, however, that things were going to change soon. The advent of night was a portent of danger, where local dogs could well shape-shift into angry badgers, baring their bloodstained fangs while mauling animals as large as bears and filleting them with their razor-sharp claws. These bloodthirsty carnivores were not to be trifled with and should be avoided at all costs. The two friends would have to switch gears, buckle up, and put on their roller skates.

CHAPTER

SEVENTEEN

As night fell, the two made their way back to the heart of the city, carefully avoiding any dark alleys or backstreets. Things were beginning to get really weird, certainly different from the mostly pleasant day they had just experienced. Lefty was able to see through the walls of buildings like an X-ray machine and could easily hear the liquids that filled the pipes therein, gurgling and splashing about. This was getting irritating, yet there was nothing he could do about it. This goddamn irresponsible drug just would not go away. They lurched back onto Duval Street just as a large eagle with a wingspan of about twelve feet came screaming toward them, feathers flying, barely giving them time to jump back on the sidewalk. Upon further inspection, they saw that this bird of prey was riding a beach cruiser, his talons keeping a death grip on the pedals and his wings not touching the handlebars. He roared away in a haze of Technicolor dust and disappeared around the corner with an ear-piercing screech that slowly faded away in the distance. Shaken, the boys decided that this should liven up Mallory Square just a bit, and maneuvered up the street toward the cruise docks. Just then, Lefty remembered that they were only a block away from the Green Parrot. It was billed as "A Sunny Place for Shady People." This, of course, piqued their interest, so they took a right on Southard Street, went one block to Whitehead and approached the entrance. Above the door was a sign that read: "No Sniveling." Feeling that they would be able to comply with this one criterion, they went in to meet their destiny.

The bar was full and they pushed their way into the mob confidently. "Hey, we *own* this place. We've been here before. We were invited here by some *very* important people. In fact, *we* are very important people. But, most importantly, we *belong* here," was repeated over and over until it seemed to be true. It was at that moment that Pancho met his vision face-to-face. She was a voluptuous beauty, tall and tanned, with rosy cheeks and long blonde hair. She also only had one arm. She said she was a go-go dancer and went by the name of Connie. Lefty had heard of many one-armed go-go girls in his lifetime, and pondered what it was that would make the profession so inherently dangerous. Pancho was in a world of bliss and immediately had to know everything about her. Lefty broke up this tete-a-tete to inquire if she would like an adult beverage. Lefty knew he liked her when she requested a double rum runner. He made his way to the bar, watched the action swirling around him, and began to relax. When it was his turn to order, he had to fall back to his nonverbal communication skills, for the noise and clamor, both inside his head and out, were beginning to exceed a comfortable level. He had become quite good at this and was quickly proffered the three cocktails he ordered. He returned to find the two new friends nearly touching noses and thoroughly engrossed in each other. Lefty smiled at his friend's good luck, and only then remembered that Pancho had first described his vision to him while on the "Eden Express." He also had said something about angel wings. Connie turned away from Lefty and pointed to a sign above the bar that read: "No Cover, No Minimum, No Wonder." He laughed to himself and then it hit him. With her back still turned to him, he saw the wings. Harley Davidson wings, to be precise. Lefty probably wouldn't have believed this if it had been related to him secondhand, but he was there when this prophecy was declared and he would be amazed until his dying day.

Speaking of dying, Lefty's back teeth were beginning to float and he would be in need of a bathroom rather quickly. He excused himself, but his words fell on deaf ears. It occurred to him that if for any reason he temporarily lost his vision, he would have hit the trifecta of being deaf, dumb, and blind, all in one day. He casually made his way to the toilet and found a short line snaking down the hall. Even at twenty paces, the stench of urine and vomit was enough to convince him that this would be unacceptable. Even as a child, Lefty had been the very proud owner of a very weak stomach. Sour milk and rotten eggs had proven to be the worst. Once, in junior high school, his great friend, Richard, had invited him to stay over for lunch after a front yard football game. Richard announced, "I think this milk is sour. Here, taste it." Ever the trusting soul, Lefty had almost drained the glass before the projectile vomiting began. He would not soon forget that experience, and retreated down the hallway quickly.

Lefty made his way back through the crowd and exited the front door. A cute local girl of about twenty-eight was standing there by herself with both hands gripping her lower jaw that seemed to be grossly protruding outward. Lefty inquired if she was in pain. She shook her head and continued to work the mutant mandible. After a moment or two, he heard a loud *pop* and her jaw was once again in its normal position. Cute had turned into beautiful and she began to explain that she was able to unhinge her jaw at will. She was able to do this fairly easily and used it to win bar bets. She reckoned that she had not paid for a drink in the last five years. The imagery of this act brought many thoughts to Lefty's now-frazzled brain and none of them were moral. They chatted for a spell until the reason for his departure from the bar reared its ugly head and he asked if there was a bathroom nearby.

"Ma'am, I truly have enjoyed our discourse," he said, trying hard to appear worldly, "but if I don't get to a suitable facility in the very near future, I just might embarrass myself. Do you know of a tree that needs watering anywhere nearby?" Lefty said, dropping the educated charade and shifting his weight from boot to boot.

"What trees are you talking about? Those palms? Around these parts, they're about the closest you're going to get. I've almost forgotten what a real tree looks like. You're kind of funny and I like the way you talk. I'm sorry about what I said; I was just playin' about the trees. We do have a few that aren't palms, just not many. My name is Jilly, and in answer to your question, my brother, Allen, is the manager of that little bistro three doors down and they have a bathroom. Right over there...see it? That *is* what you were asking about, wasn't it?"

Lefty's floating eyeballs followed her slender arm that pointed up the street and he saw a sign above a door that read: "The Dead Dolphin." Lefty thought to himself that it was an odd name for a bistro, but nevertheless asked, "Ummm, why don't you wait right here and..."

Jilly rolled her eyes, waiting for the upcoming pickup line that seemed to be marching down Main Street waving a flag right about now.

Lefty finished by saying, "I'll see if you were lying about all that 'bar bet' business."

She was pleasantly surprised by the statement, and replied, "Well, okay. But you better hurry up and get on with it because I might just have other fish to fry, you know." She leaned against a low wall and said to Lefty as he hurriedly limped away, "Allen's a little queer, in an island kind of way, but he doesn't bite like I do. You tell him that I sent you. There shouldn't be a problem."

Lefty thought about this. *Shouldn't be a problem? Bite like I do? Holy mother of God. What next?* He ambled down the serene backstreet while contemplating this simple twist of fate.

As he approached the door of the bistro, something caught his attention. Just down the street, an intense eye peered at him from around the corner, just like Pinkie would do at home when she wanted to be invisible. The body that owned this eye seemed to be wearing some sort of cape and a tricornered hat. Looking decidedly like a buccaneer of old, the eye never blinked. Slowly, almost imperceptibly, the orb disappeared from Lefty's view. He shrugged it off and found his way to the men's room, thinking little of this relatively mundane sight amid the rest of the bizarre visions he'd had since getting off the bus. He hurriedly found a stall and let loose the flood. This was certainly a relief and he let out an audible sigh. Looking down, Lefty was shocked all the way to his boots. His urine stream had become a Roman candle of shooting stars and sparks of vibrant colors. The walls began to crawl and his hands became clammy. Not sure of what to make of this, and certainly hoping against all hope that this fireworks display didn't end with a loud bang as his penis exploded, Lefty explored the idea of dropping to his knees and extinguishing this firework display in the bowl. Luckily, the flames disappeared and he tried to calm himself. He left the stall and carefully washed his hands. Grabbing a hand towel, he looked up and found himself staring into the abyss—a mirror.

Before this adventure began, the two pals had decided that there would be three hard-and-fast rules that they would adhere to at all times. The first was that no timepieces were to be used at any time. The second was that they were not to split up. The third and most important rule was never to come in contact with a mirror. They were evil and could pull you inside of them for long periods of time. But it was too late. Lefty found himself locked in its grip and was paralyzed by its strength. He noticed that his pupils had become large and were taking in things unforeseen until now. Every blemish, pore, and imperfection on his face radiated through his brain. He carefully examined his hands, which were still clammy, and saw that they were again weathered and chapped. His hair had become a fright-wig made of straw and his appearance had taken on the qualities of an ancient Mexican peasant. He examined his caricature with great care for what seemed like eons. With horror, he wondered what he had become. Unexpectedly, the door was thrown open and the spell was broken. The manager sashayed in, mostly to see what had become of the Texan. They exchanged awkward nods and Lefty quickly left the establishment.

As he neared the Parrot, Lefty spied a caped figure disappearing into the shadows. Seeing that Jilly had not waited as promised, Lefty ran to the spot where the mysterious figure had evaporated. All he found was a smoldering foreign cigarette and some strange paw prints. This might soon become a cause for concern, but for now Lefty had other things to attend to and some apologies to make. He once again entered the Parrot.

Pancho was not hard to spot, even in this throng. As usual, he had drawn a crowd and was telling wild, ribald tales from the past. His booming voice led Lefty to believe that things were beginning to return to normal, but for how long? As he made his way toward him, he scanned the crowd for Jilly. Not seeing her, he tried to spit out an explanation as he approached the couple. Apparently, his absence had not been noticed and he hurriedly ordered another round. Shortly after, Connie excused herself and made her way to the bathroom. Lefty thought of warning her, but she was a local and certainly knew the condition of the facilities.

Pancho grabbed Lefty in a chokehold and yelled at him for leaving. "Where have you been, you son of a bitch? I thought we had some fast-and-cool rules in place here or whatever. Right there on page one, you little shit. Open up that goddamn journal and see for yourself," Pancho growled at him, with his eyes bulging from their sockets. After a moment, he regained his composure and asked exactly where Lefty had gone for the nearly hour and a half. Lefty wasn't sure he wanted to fess up to having broken not one, but two of the fiats agreed to by the both of them, when Pancho forgot what they were talking about and announced that someone was looking for him. He had been having such a good time with his new companion that he, too, had lost track of time until a beautiful girl named Jilly approached them and asked if they were friends of Lefty's. He went on to say that it had happened only about five minutes ago and she had said they might meet up tomorrow after she got off work. Lefty was ecstatic. Unfortunately for Pancho, it was also now time for his go-go dancer to report for work. With a warm one-armed hug, she said that they would all meet again the following day.

As she walked away, Connie said over her shoulder, "Lefty, you'll like Jilly. She's not like the others. She's experienced."

Pancho shot his pal a "You just got lucky, Lefty" look and patted Connie on her rear end as she fled the scene.

With warm hearts, they made their way to the bar and, incredibly, found two seats. After ordering, they spoke of the good fortune that had befallen them and of what tomorrow might bring. Suddenly, an errant elbow was jabbed into Pancho's ribs. He was unaccustomed to this sort of treatment and, slowly turning his head, glared over his shoulder. The elbow was still digging into his rib cage, yet there was no one in immediate sight doing the poking. He lowered his gaze to see a peculiar man wearing thick glasses and sporting a pompadour. Without removing his pointy elbow, he yelled at the barman for an orange soda. Thankfully, Pancho found this almost amusing, for he could easily cripple this fellow with just a simple backhand. This miscreant loudly proclaimed to be a physician of sorts and began to espouse his beliefs about the world's demon—rum. He was clearly intoxicated, it was just not apparent from what. Lefty tried to remember the lyrics to a song he had heard Willie Nelson sing a hundred times before, but just wasn't sure if he had the phrasing right. Undecided, he blurted out awkwardly, "There are more old drunks than there are old doctors, so I guess we better have another round." They both laughed at the absurdity of the situation and took Willie's advice.

A happy Pancho announced he was hungry and perhaps tiring a bit. They agreed it was, indeed, time to eat. They had fed their heads all day and it was time to feed their bellies. They made their way to the door, and after getting their bearings, turned toward the depot to retrieve their belongings from the locker.

Pancho was the gastronomical genius of the two, so he was in charge of the menu tonight. Lefty's head was still swirling, just with not as much centrifugal force as before, and was content to follow his pal to wherever he was led. Considering their location, fish and lobster seemed to be a logical choice so they made their way to the marina.

Marinas at night are magical places. Island music, steel drums and soca, or soul/Caribbean music, would fill the night air with their polyrhythmic beats, and there was always a lot of dancing. Blenders were never empty as they dispensed the tropical social lubricants so familiar to those from island locales. There was also never a shortage of food, because each boat normally returned with several species of fish and crustaceans, so much so that it was communally shared. After a few of these strong, lethal cocktails, everyone became best friends and bonds were formed, if only for the night.

At the end of the longest dock was a group livelier than the rest. Pancho, always able to sniff out a good party, led the way down the wooden planks to see what the hubbub was about. Captain G. held a nightly after-sunset soirée there on the docks where the local fishermen would gather to eat the day's catch. It evidently had been a bountiful day on the water for all involved and everyone was in great spirits. Captain G. was the ringleader of this circus and kept his freaks in line with the lash of his mordant tongue.

Lefty's plan was to see if anyone needed a person skilled with a fillet knife so they might be able to work off their dinner instead of paying for it. Luckily for the two, all the fish had been prepared and the shellfish had been boiled or steamed. It was lucky because, at this point, Lefty had no business being in charge of anything so finely honed as a fillet knife.

"Come aboard, boys. There is good grub and stiff drink available for everyone tonight. The sea was a tramp today and she gave us her all!" This was a cause for guffaws and back-slapping among the partiers, and Lefty and Pancho immediately made themselves at home.

Lefty felt as if he had met a friend from another lifetime in Captain G. They hit it off immediately and the two Texans were greeted like warriors returning from battle, which was a pretty fair description of their day. After accepting a couple of ostentatiously large and colorful boat drinks, they were passed two paper plates and two plastic forks by a young lady of considerable girth who still wore her bikini. This "girth" referred to her enormous bustline that was presently incarcerated by what appeared to be mouse dental floss. Trying not to stare, they eagerly filled their plates and found two sling-back chairs made of blue cotton cloth featuring sailboats of all descriptions. They were entirely comfortable when they slipped off their boots and slid deeply into the chairs. Dinner was an exquisite feast of dolphin and grouper stew, a light, crisp salad, and warm sourdough bread. Seconds were offered, but their firsts had been more than enough. Now sated, Captain G. and his lovely new bride extended them Chilean wine and Cuban cigars that finished this epicurean banquet. The wine was a particularly nice touch to smooth out some tangled neurons.

"Where are you boys planning on bunking for the night? There's room here on *The Keylypso* if you don't mind the banshee wailing of my new bride while I have a go at her. She's a wildcat after a cocktail or two...heavy on the *cock* and *tail*, I must admit!"

The two didn't have to think for long, and Lefty said simply, "I think that tonight is a good night for some stargazing, and we wouldn't want to be a bother, anyway. I mean, you've already been kind enough to let two malcontents like us on board in the first place."

"Well, if you change your minds you know where the doorbell is. Looks like you have a majestic night for some celestial viewing. Maybe you'll come by tomorrow and we'll take a cruise in this rust bucket. Might get lucky and grab one of those big blues you were talking about earlier. Anyway, y'all have a safe night and be careful. You never know what's out there on a night like tonight."

Lefty's head now was envisioning reeling in the great marlin like his mentor had done so long ago. Now that would *really* be an adventure to add to his growing journal.

As they waved good-bye, a firework went off in the distant sky. It traveled in an arc before turning into a gigantic red lotus flower that glittered back to Earth in slow motion, and it sort of summed up their day. Or did it? Was this trip over, or just beginning?

Returning to Duval Street, they turned south, away from the madness that was just now reaching a fevered crescendo, and followed it until it dead-ended into South Beach. Just to the east was Dog Beach, which was never a choice, for there might be leftovers from an un-curbed canine underneath their heads as they slept. Making sure to stay above the high-water mark of tidal action, they made themselves comfortable using the backpack as a pillow.

Away from the lights of town, the sky was ablaze with stars and other celestial spangles. Some were red, some blue, but most were white and twinkled like car lights on a rainy highway. Some flew across the sky looking for new homes while others were cemented in place and pulsed like beating hearts. They enjoyed the show for a few minutes and then, exhausted, they fell into a deep slumber.

CHAPTER EIGHTEEN

It was still dark when Lefty awoke. He felt remarkably refreshed, even after what only amounted to a nap. Perhaps it was the comforting lull of the waves, or maybe it was the wonderful dinner they had enjoyed the night before that had persuaded this rejuvenating repose. Lefty reached for Pancho, only to find him gone. This was not disturbing to him, for Pancho didn't require a lot of sleep, and at home would often wander around the house in his slippers and little else looking for something to hold his interest. Late-night television was over after the news wrap-up that followed Johnny Carson. That is, except for one religious program featuring a very effeminate evangelist named Jim Baker, who had no visible lips, and his wife, who wore cheap clown makeup that would run down her face every time she praised the Lord in thanksgiving. Brother Baker, as he preferred to be addressed, reminded Lefty of the Sunday morning cartoon of his youth called *Clutch Cargo*. On this particular show, the characters were entirely animated except for their mouths. A real human mouth read the dialogue through a slit in the animation that left no room for lips. Lefty had always found this infinitely more interesting than the Claymation of *Davey and Goliath* and its right-wing religious pandering.

Nonetheless, Pancho had taken leave and Lefty would have to stand guard over the camp for now. He had enjoyed the night under the stars, because it reminded him of going to camp when he was a young man. He had cherished those summer days and nights spent in the Hill Country outside of Austin like no others, and to this day would dream about them.

Without warning, a cat howled, and as it faded away to a low plaint, the hair on Lefty's body felt like it began to stand on end. He envisioned it being a rare Florida panther with sharp, muscular claws dripping with blood rather than the just plain dune cat that it probably was. If there were only a little more light besides the occasional strobe-flash of heat lightning off in the distance, he might try to scribble down a few thoughts.

Soon, the first pink rays of dawn grew from the horizon to his left. Against a backdrop of lessening blue, yellow shards of light filtered their way to the heavens. In the growing illumination, he was able to make out large banks of cumulus clouds in the distance due south from his perch. This would turn out not to be heat lightning at all, but rather a tempest brewing offshore. As far as he could tell, the storm was moving parallel to the coast and posed no danger to them.

Pancho suddenly appeared, with his arms filled with various citrus fruit he had pilfered from some low-hanging branches along a back-street. His hands were bleeding from his attempt to strip a key lime tree of its prized fruit, having been unaware that the branches held thorns that would rival any rose bush or bougainvillea. Lefty pulled out one of his bandanas and helped wipe the blood off the oranges and red grapefruits.

Pancho mentioned that he had passed a public bathroom and was going to head back to use it. Lefty needed to urinate but was afraid of another fireworks explosion, and thought it might be better to wade out in the water just in case he needed to extinguish the flames quickly. He might even be able to rinse off some of the road grime he had been collecting.

When Pancho returned, he pulled out the razor-sharp Bowie and carefully cut up the fruit. He then licked the blade clean and attentively returned it to its sheath. The freshness of the fruit was amazing, and soon their chins glistened with the juicy pulp that had escaped their eager lips. After finishing the snack, they walked to the water's edge, dipped their sticky fingers into the surf, and washed them carefully. Their faces were next, and soon they too were relatively clean. The crispness of the salty ocean water contrasted with the heat that emanated from their unquestionably sun-kissed faces and it made them feel healthy, strong, and alive.

In the few short minutes they had spent there on the strand, the tide had reclaimed another foot of beach and the shore break was intensifying at a forbidding pace. Lefty once again peered out at the horizon and saw that the Gulf Stream had grown into a wall of water that easily held waves of twelve feet or more just a mile offshore. This body of water traversed the southern part of Florida and Cuba before heading up the eastern coast of the United States. A storm was unusual for this time of year and could be a portent of dangerous weather forming in the Florida Straits. And it would assuredly change the shape of their day with Captain G.

Lefty and Pancho sat facing each other after consuming the second, and last, body of the sacrament needed to complete this epic passage. They each looked into the soul of the other, hoping to discover a part of themselves in which they were deficient. As their pupils ballooned and the nausea withdrew, these thoughts were shelved and they prepared to decamp. Once more, the mystic fog enfolded them and the adventure began anew.

The friends were fairly confident that the experience gained from the previous day would help guide them through the peaks and valleys that lay before them today, so they gathered their belongings, put them in the backpack, and trudged single-file across the damp sand to the dunes. Pancho found a fish skeleton and tried, unsuccessfully, to comb his matted hair, finally throwing it away in disgust. A path cut through the trampled dune grass and sea grapes led them back to town, where they made a beeline to the depot to unburden themselves of the nonessentials. Happy to find an empty locker, they made their way to a bench where they would decide on a tactical plan for the day.

Knowing the danger of another mirror encounter, they groomed each other like the Capuchin monkeys they had seen in various zoos around the world, trying to make themselves presentable in this tropical Valhalla. Lefty had always liked these primates, except for the time one had flung some steaming dung at his head and, to put it politely, its aim had been true. Lefty had thrown the turd back, causing a great commotion with the monkeys, who vocalized their displeasure quite loudly while they swung madly around the gigantic cage. This grooming ceremony had drawn a crowd that embarrassed Lefty to no end, and since he wasn't looking for a repeat of the poop-flinging incident, he shooed Pancho's monkey fingers away. Luckily, this was Key West and only a small crowd had formed to watch this drollery. They were quiet for the most part when Pancho stood and announced to the gathered proletariat that the next show would begin at noon, and they hurriedly made their way to the marina.

Things had drastically changed overnight at the docks. While the streets still possessed the lunacy of a normal day, the marina had become almost a vacant parking lot, and what boats remained were being attended to with a frenzy of activity. The serenity and gaiety of the night before was gone in the glare of the new morning. Lefty led the way to *The Keylypso* and found Captain G. with a worried look on his face. He was busy tying down the bow and stern lines to their respective cleats after already securing the spring lines.

"Good morning, Captain!" Lefty shouted as they came alongside the vessel. Lefty had been around enough boats to know that something was up and asked permission to come aboard.

"I see you boys survived the evening," Captain G. said gruffly. "It doesn't look like we will be doing any gaffing of those marlin any time soon. Mother Ocean woke up on the wrong side of the cat box today. Take off those boots and climb aboard."

Pancho was relieved, and said, "I'm not much for the open seas, anyway. Need some help?"

Lefty posed the obvious question next, "Does it look like something's happening out there? I mean, something that might be a problem for us? And just where in the hell does everyone go during a big storm?"

"Not much gets by you two, I'll say that much. Yeah, we're gonna get wet. She's gathering strength right out there," the captain said, pointing to the south.

While not officially the time of year for a hurricane, every so often a storm would develop outside the parameters of this so-called "season" and catch everyone off guard. These freak storms left little time for preparation other than taking the normal marine precautions. Lefty had heard around that the "men in the desert," or the Vegas boys who figured out such things for those so inclined, had laid the odds at one to two that the two Texans would return home unscathed from this misadventure, but the emerging situation could and would drastically change those odds.

Captain G. had been a lifelong Conch, as Key West residents referred to themselves, and had ridden out many storms, both at sea and ashore. He had decided that this storm would be what was designated as a "rain event." Most of the other boats had not heeded his prediction and would try to outrun this deviant rain shower.

"Well, alright then!" Pancho said finally, relaxed with the knowledge that a veteran seaman such as Captain G. would ride this one out. "There must be *something* we can do to help out around here, though. And just where is that new bride of yours, anyway? Is she still recovering from those 'cocktails' you fed her last night?"

The captain looked at the two lecherously and said, "She might be a little sore, but she's well enough to make it to the market for the necessities and such. She was limping a bit crooked today, but we've already boarded up the hovel this morning and are good to go, so the only thing I've really got to do is lug some of this tackle up to the truck so I can get it over to the warehouse. Here, gimme a hand."

The weighty toting of the marine gear and portable generator was accomplished with the three of them joining forces, despite the fact that Lefty and Pancho did have some trouble navigating their way back to the truck at times. This was due to their lack of ambulatory coordination caused by the earlier ceremonial rite, but shortly everything was ready for transfer.

On the way to the warehouse, the seaman explained to Lefty and Pancho about what made a Conch tick. He said they all seemed to possess an inherent and essential character trait that would make them risk their lives to reside here in fairy-tale land. They found it interesting that most islanders, unless being faced with the real threat of a direct hit from a strong storm, were more inclined to throw a party rather than leave. Each resident had what were referred to as "hidey-holes" that were shelters from the wind and rain. The locations were secret and normally not shared with one another. This brought an air of mystery to Lefty's already reeling brain, and he began to imagine revolving bookcases that led to well-stocked basements and trapdoors that led to bomb shelters. Unfortunately, he had forgotten to take into consideration that the island sat on sand and an underground chamber of any sort would be almost impossible to create.

They arrived at the storage unit and found that the entire truck could fit inside the deceivingly large compartment. Inside, the cinderblock walls were braced by what appeared to be four-by-fours and had empty shelving that would hold the boating and fishing gear well off the ground. As they filled the shelves directly from the back of the truck, Pancho surmised that they had probably seen their first "hidey-hole" and made a mental note of the location.

Padlocking the door after backing out the truck, Captain G. stretched and asked, "Now that the weather's gone south, what are you two knuckleheads going to do with your time today? You both look like you are on planet Xeron already, and that alone makes for a perfect fit around these here parts. I thought you said you might be hooking up with a couple of dollies later."

This reminded Pancho's "other head" of Connie, and he adjusted himself while saying, "No, we're going to meet up with them a little later. It might be time to take a listen to a marine radio for the latest update, though. Do you know where we can find one, G.?"

The three looked at the sky for several moments and saw the first dark clouds fly by at brisk speeds that bespoke of later disturbances, which, for now, would be ignored.

The seaman finally said, "Yeah, I know a place. Come on." They drove away to the cacophonous sound of the crushing of thousands of prehistoric shell fragments. Fortuitously, he pulled up in front of a run-down tavern that was frequented by the lower tier of local fishermen and apparently went by the name "BAR."

As the trio disembarked from the truck, Lefty and Pancho realized that they had again boarded the roller coaster and it was leaving the platform. Breathing had become of particular interest to them, as they could feel the damp air enter their mouths, circulate down the windpipe and swirl into their lungs. From there, it would continue to wriggle through the alveoli until it was sucked back out and banished once again to the outside world. Lefty was convinced that he could clearly hear this entire process in his head and would need to concentrate closely to ensure that he didn't forget this respiration blueprint, thereby passing out on the ground and dying a slow and painful death. The upside to this looming danger was the appearance of large amounts of adrenaline that shot through his body and kept one leg moving in front of the other. The pressure in his chest melted for the moment and he followed the captain inside through the broken screen door.

Captain G. was greeted like royalty while a table was instantly cleared and, seeing that he had company, a checkered tablecloth was thrown on the rickety table to complete the baronial effect. Normally, he commanded a seat at the bar and held court, but today he wished to sit near the quaint, if not outdated, marine radio to wait for the next report.

The boys quietly sat down and examined the new surroundings. The walls were stark, with the exception of a lone, moth-eaten tarpon that had had the misfortune to have swallowed the hook of a drunken taxidermist. It was missing an eye and several of its shiny scales. The smells found here were not unexpected and generally consisted of stale beer and fusty rags. Their aural awareness was working at peak levels, but unfortunately the comprehension and translation of these sounds and conversations had fallen several lengths behind and were not gaining any ground. Lefty assumed he had not lost his tongue again, it just had not occurred to him to try and use it yet after their arrival. The imposing captain ordered dark rum with tonic, double lime, and looked over at the Texans. They glanced at each other before Pancho blurted that they would have the same. He had correctly decided that "when in Rome..."

When the drinks arrived, Pancho flinched and threw a scowl in Lefty's direction. Noting the tiny flotsam that bobbed on the surface of this rum concoction, Lefty observed the lack of sanitary cleaning stations and then looked at the riffraff that made up the clientele. He decided that it would be a judgment call on whether or not to quaff this beverage. They had made it this far, so he took a long, slow gulp and hoped for the best. Pancho seemed relieved that his pal did not foam at the mouth and he cautiously took a small sip. Feeling no ill effect, Lefty removed his straw and began to chew it furiously to keep from grinding his teeth. This gnashing had become a problem because his jaws were still sore from this same experience yesterday. The drinks were unusually stout and made Lefty's eyes water. He decided that when he found his way home, he would return to his juice and herbal tea regimen and give his liver a rest. Of course, he wasn't home yet, so he gave the universal sign of another round for the table and tried to remember to breathe.

The radio abruptly spat out a cross fire of static across the table that rattled the ice cubes in the tumblers in front of them. Shaken, the boys hoped that the others didn't notice how their fingers trembled as they tried to smooth the hair on the nape of their necks back into its original location. As Lefty downed his drink and ordered another, he stole a glance out the screen door and saw a caped figure with the familiar tricornered hat race by steering a vintage Italian Piaggio Vespa down the unpaved road. As the phantom sped by, he tossed something on the ground and smiled a devilish leer. This was becoming a cause of concern for Lefty, until he heard the troublesome weather forecast come through the worn transistors. Ostensibly, the storm had made a move to the north and had become tropical. This meant a greater chance for more wind and rain than Captain G. had earlier predicted and left the boys in the more precarious position of having to decide sooner, rather than later, on their next move. The seaman tried to calm them a bit by ordering yet another round and reassuring them that the storm was still actually more than a day and a half away.

Looking around the barroom, Pancho noticed that everyone seemed to be quite calm as all watched the battered TV with snow on its screen. He wondered if the other patrons knew that there was no picture until the barkeep looked up, moved the rabbit ears slightly, and the blizzard seemed to dissipate a bit for the time being, clearing the way for *Let's Make a Deal* to make a groggy appearance. Lefty continued to watch the road for an assault from the cunning pirate.

An hour later, Lefty gave Pancho the high sign and, as they prepared to leave, the bill was brought to the table. It was remarkably cheap, and as Lefty and Pancho tried to pull out some currency, a large hand rose angrily in the air, slapped the table and covered the tab, then leisurely pulled back the now-crumpled paper.

"Now just what in the hell do you think you are doing?" Captain G. bellowed. "No friend of mine *ever* pays for drinks, at least as long as I am upright! Now put those dead presidents back in that pocket of yours or I'll release the hounds. And I don't want to hear a word out of either of you, you hear?"

He walked them to the door and followed them to the curb-less street. He leaned an elbow on the back of the truck and smiled at his two new friends. "Hey, calm down, I didn't mean to scare you. I always cause a fuss when that happens. I've got a 'Bwana Willie' image to maintain with those no-account deckhands and I've got to keep my street cred up, you know. Hell, I never pay the damn bill, anyway. I just bring the owner back a shitload of fish from time to time and we're all square."

He wrote his pertinent numbers on the back of an unblemished business card given to him by a bail bondsman that had come down from Miami to do some permit fishing and, thinking he would never make it that far north, much less in need of a bondsman, handed the card over and sped off with a shrill "Ooo-whee!" and a cloud of tailpipe smoke.

As they turned toward town, Lefty became aware of the butt of a Djarum cigarette that lay among the crushed shells and wondered what the chances were that he would find a clove cigarette in this tropical locale. Catching up with Pancho, they noticed a tiny collection of what appeared to be full-grown deer, except for the fact that they only came up to Pancho's knees. They resembled miniature white-tails, and while none appeared to pose any immediate danger to the duo, they made no hasty or furtive moves in their direction. Cautiously, they gave them a wide berth before changing gears and narrowly escaping. The friends looked at each other and knew that the landscape was becoming very strange, indeed.

Back in the burg, the friends discovered that the circus that was the Grateful Dead had pulled into town overnight and had begun to assemble their tents. Pancho had taken Lefty to his first Dead show a few years prior and it had been an eye-opening initiation for him. The music was mesmerizing, but the crowd that followed the band made it the experience that it was. In fact, for those that were unable to obtain a "miracle ticket" to a particular venue, the parking lot scene had become almost as good as the show itself, with the buying and selling of strange, organic sandwiches and colorful clothing, among other things. Happily, the buddies discovered that tonight was an off night for the band and, being in the area, it was decided that the group would drop by this decadent oasis and give a free show on the beach. This immediately raised the chi of the two pals, although not their ability to communicate more than a few words at a time, so they followed the crowds to the party on Duval, letting their souls and spirits sail into the mystic once again.

Because of the predicted storm, no cruise ships were in port today, allowing the locals to do what they do best—freak freely. Fans of the band took to the streets in large numbers, exploring the island in long-haired packs. There was not a single soul on the avenue that wasn't smiling a broad, toothy grin. Their colorful clothing was a source of constant delight for the two boys, who by now had taken seats on the curb to monitor the activities. People seemed to think they knew everyone and strangers would stop just to shake their hand. It was a definite change of atmosphere from the preceding day and much more to their liking, as they felt like they had become part of the community. Pretty girls would come and go, sometimes chatting for a while. They seemed to be so natural and free, as opposed to the "undertaker makeup" look that had painted the garish tourist hordes from the day before.

Pancho had somehow managed to verbalize to one of these young angels the earlier sighting of the heinous pocket-sized deer and wondered if they had been seeing things out of the ordinary. She explained that they were indeed dwarfs called Key deer, and then laughed as she asked to have some of whatever he had ingested. She giggled coyly as she looked over her shoulder on the way back to her heaven, the wind fluidly rippling her sundress and auburn hair. This reminded Lefty of the meeting with Jilly and Connie that surely must be coming up, but since they possessed no timepieces, they would have to estimate the time. Pancho guessed that the appointment was still at least an hour away, which was fine with Lefty, as he was becoming one with the curb.

Things looked to be going along just fine until Lefty felt his body flash with heat and then become numb. He watched what appeared to be his brain liquefy, run down his face, drip to the ground and seep into the storm drain. This stunning vision momentarily paralyzed him with fear, only to be followed by a sense of balance and harmonic well-being. As he processed this horrific, yet engaging, phantasmal illusion, he came to the realization that he had just shed his old brain, making way for a new one, like when snakes slough off their old skins. It was a kind of a rebirth or baptism and his mind was again fresh and revitalized. He scribbled furiously in the diary about this event, going into great detail while he still had lucid recall.

He nudged Pancho and succinctly relayed the tale to his friend, whose eyes became grossly enlarged as he listened. When he finished the story, Pancho let out an audible sigh of relief.

"Holy shit! I just had the same damn thing happen to me. I swear, I thought I literally had my brain dripping out of my ears. It almost felt good...almost. Wasn't like a bad thing, you know. I felt like I was losing all the garbage that had been collecting there over the years, things that

I knew were bad, like cleansing my body and soul from the top to the bottom. I feel like a new person and I already see things in a new light. And there were other things; I just can't remember them right now. For a minute there, I thought I was going crazy, but *no, no, no*! I was becoming sane."

With this episode now out in the open, a lively discussion began and was only interrupted when two beautiful girls named Jilly and Connie came up and reprimanded them before joining them on the sidewalk.

CHAPTER
NINETEEN

The girls had waited like pigeons on a monu-
ment at the Parrot for quite some time before
deciding to search for the boys. It had been easy
to spot them because of the crowd that had
assembled to witness the loud roundtable debate
that arose from the curb and had spread across
the street. Pancho and Lefty looked at the swarm
sheepishly, only then realizing that a crowd had
even assembled. It was also the moment that the
sun broke through the clouds to say hello for
the first time since that morning, and after Lefty
and Pancho greeted the girls, the four strode to
a nearby groggery in a grand mood.

As the group discussed the day's events, Lefty
watched the girls closely. Although extremely
happy at home, he was in need of some female
companionship now and he appreciated the fact
they had come across these two when they
did. Jilly wore gardenias in her hair, Connie had

jasmine, and this added to the fresh bouquet that filled the air that often precedes a storm. The girls had both stated that they were in relationships so there would be no dalliances, and this was begrudgingly accepted by the two friends. It would have been far more unusual for them not to have been involved, considering their charm and desirability, so they were flattered that the girls would even show up in the first place.

Jilly soon tapped Lefty on the shoulder and told him that it looked like someone was watching them from the alley across the street. He turned to look and spied the familiar hat-and-one-eye-around-the-corner figure that had been hounding them. Lefty excused himself and made his way to the door, but the eye had slowly evaporated once again. Crossing the street, he searched for any sign of the Vespa. Finding none, he returned and sat at the table with a bedeviled look on his face.

The conversation had taken a strange turn in his absence. The girls were opening the religious box that housed Pandora with the precept that if there was no disbelief in life, there would inherently be no faith. Pancho tried to put a political slant on this somehow, while all Lefty could think about was why this nut job on a foreign scooter was tracking them like wounded bison. Had they somehow insulted a local dignitary? And why the eccentric pirate outfit? He knew some weirdoes back in Austin that might do something like this, but here? Not wanting to panic, he explained that he needed to see another man about another horse. He found the water closet—which was truly that, a closet—behind the small bar and popped in, only to come face-to-face with a mirror. He jumped out of the way before it could draw him into its grasp and locked himself in a stall. He silently thanked his parents for not passing on the claustrophobia gene and settled in to watch the pyrotechnic show. It was more spectacular this time, and he found himself clapping along with the rest of the imagined crowd during the grand finale. This clapping, unfortunately, left nothing to man the "hose" with, and he used his shirttail to try and dry his now soaked jeans.

Trying to remember how long he had been gone, and not wanting the word to spread to the girls of his fiery urinary disorder, he hurried back to the table and unobtrusively sat down. Jilly was voicing how she had always wanted to be considered an enthusiast rather than a tour- ist, when she scooted her chair closer to Lefty. She reached under the table and held his hand, interlacing her fingers through his. This was a wonderful gesture and it immediately calmed him. She leaned and whispered in his ear, "Just hang on to me and you will be alright." She had evi- dently been on this ride before and was guiding him through the peaks.

Pancho rose to his feet and threw his arms in the air. "If that isn't the damnedest thing. The good old Grateful Dead playing on the beach tonight. And for *free*! I simply cannot tell you what an event this will be. We are exactly in the right place at the right time in the universe." By this time, Pancho was circling the table, slapping the other three on the back, throwing waves to the other patrons and generally doing what he did best—being excited about life. "Yes sir...and ladies," he said, doffing an imaginary bowler, "we are in for the time of our young lives. There's no doubt about it! This will be the piece de résistance, the fin de siecle. Without all that self-doubt part, you know. There is absolutely no other place in history that I'd rather be than right here in Key West with my fine friends and all that that entails. Even the Romans and their wild-ass orgies had nothing on this!"

Pancho finally collapsed in a nearby chair and tooted. The gas evidently wasn't leaving, but the group decided they would.

They rose from their seats, holding their noses to keep out the malodorous stench that in no way reminded anyone of strawberry ice cream, and ambled down to the bus station to retrieve the tequila and limes and to drop off the diary, before heading to the shore to check out the craziness. They all walked hand in hand on the busy street, knowing there was nothing of which they needed to be ashamed. As the four found the beach and all that came with this spectacle, they were amazed at the energy surging through, in, and around the crowd. A large stage had been erected perpendicular to the beach, with the crowd extending as far as the eye could see. Further out from the sand, tents had been set up and small campfires were pocketed here and there. The girls saw several friends around one fire who invited them to hang out for a while. They were offered a special tea, which they enjoyed, although it had a sort of a familiar fungal taste. Lefty and his nether regions were flattered that Jilly never let go of his hand, even in front of all her girlfriends.

He felt the tea take effect as the clouds began to zoom across the darkening sky and a chill crept into the passing breezes. He noticed that Jilly's nipples were staring at his eyes, and every time he would look away, they would still be ogling him when his gaze returned. It was beginning to become uncomfortable for him and he wanted to ask why her breasts were still leering at him, when she caught him with a playful punch. They laughed and hugged like old friends before settling in two aluminum folding chairs. He was at complete ease and wanted only for Dixie, as she would have fit in famously with this bunch and he was missing her.

The depth of the fun and excitement that filled the night was hard to describe. Lefty felt that he had been reduced to smiling, sighing, and murmuring to himself. He watched the crowd as they moved in and out of his field of vision, shadow figures twirling to the roar of the crowd while shapes and forms changed at will. They had traveled a long journey to this Mother Ocean, only to discover what they did not know and bear witness to what they had not seen. They had tripped into this cosmic pothole and were climbing their way back out with a valise filled with knowledge and experiences that had eluded them until this very moment.

Jilly climbed into his lap and began to purr. She was warm and soft and her nipples gouged his chest. Freed by the knowledge that nothing intimate would happen between these two, they were free to tease and flirt all they wanted. They heard the sailor's mournful cry, smelled the sea and felt the sky. It was astounding and almost incomprehensible to understand, much less explain, the profundity of this occasion. The sharing of a mystical, spiritual quest with someone, par-ticularly a new acquaintance, could forge bonds stronger than steel and last a lifetime. He had already experienced this with Pancho and was now accepting this tea party confederacy into the circle. He tried to assimilate these thoughts, but was only able to decide that his soul was about to explode with feelings of love and goodwill.

The snuggling was about to reach a new level when the stage announcer heralded the start of the party. Lefty wondered if he knew that the party had already been going on for hours as he held Jilly for maybe the last time. He would have been happy to stay at the tea party with her friends, but, although you could see the stage at a harsh angle, he knew Pancho well enough to grasp the concept of "front and center." It was decided that they would move in shifts back and forth between their camp and the actual show. Lefty was ecstatic at the notion of spending more time with the group, but he wanted to see how things were going with Pancho, so they took the first "watch," promising to try and bring back more wood for the fire. The girls were left alone and had gathered in a huddle as they left. He heard them say something about some whipped cream and a car battery before they burst out in giggles. Lefty concluded he would have loved to have been a fly on that wall as they moved out into the shadow-lands that lay between the camp and the show.

CHAPTER TWENTY

As they shuffled through the low scrub, Pancho proclaimed that this might possibly be the most fun he had ever had, and Lefty was quick to agree. He tried to explain to Lefty the myriad of images and impressions that ran through his mind like a pre1930s stock ticker spitting out tape.

"Lefty, this is the most wonderful I have ever felt in my life." Pancho was now talking in little more than whispers, and went on to say, "It is the craziest, most wonderful feeling knowing that we are on this journey together. Man, this shit comes and goes, but when it comes, look out! Take that guy over there...the one that looks like he's a human light bulb. His head is the size of a basketball and all lit up while his whole body wouldn't fill a shoebox. He's as fucked up as we are, maybe more. Is that a walrus he's standing on? Looks like it to me... And what in the *hell* are those nuns doing in a place like this? Maybe we should go over and ask them about the Bible. Like, who is this Gideon person? And what's up with that trumpet business? Lord, I have so many questions to ask them! I always thought I had all the answers and now I mostly have questions. Do you think the world is flat? It seems like we'd fall off it if it were round. I kind of like this, you know, being curious for once. I wonder what is going on back in Texas…" His voice trailed off as he fell into a chasm of new perceptions.

The band must have noticed the barometric energy in the Florida air this night and exploded into full-tilt boogie mode from the opening number. It was impossible not to dance and groove as they made their way through the crowd that stood moving and singing with the music. As they moved forward, they had to tiptoe around the various blankets and towels that quilted the ground, making sure not to kick up too much sand or step on toes. As usual, Pancho used his bulk to spearhead their advance until they found a comfortable spot near one of the sound towers. With the spotlights aimed at the stage, the low clouds that continued to streak past formed a patchwork roof over their heads and seemed to enclose them inside with the powerful music swirling all around them.

Leaning against one of the braces that supported this wall of sound, Lefty felt the electricity explode through his body; his arms and legs were alive and tingling, causing him to tremble with utter joy. He was aware of every follicle of hair on his body as they stood to be counted, and discovered that his hands had found their way to his face, more or less depicting Edvard Munch's familiar painting *The Scream*, the only difference being that he was overcome by euphoric ecstasy instead of existential angst. His ears were suddenly filled with the lyrics coming from the stage.

> *Once in a while you get shone the light,*
> *In the strangest of places if you look at it right.*

His head swirled as the panoramic vista of scarlet begonias and beautiful girls swept across his line of vision, put his brain in a stranglehold and washed to his feet. Everything was electric, animated, and breathing. Time had lost all meaning for the moment as he raced toward the light. He watched through his fingers as fantastic colors danced around and pulsed to the rhythmic beat of the percussion concussion. This went on for what seemed to be ages before the wave washed away and the song ended.

Slowing things down for a moment, the band moved into a slow, bluesy Willie Dixon song. Lefty remembered a Ralph Ellison quote that the blues were "an impulse to keep the painful details and episodes of a brutal experience alive in one's aching consciousness, to finger its jagged grain, and to transcend it, not by the consolation of philosophy but by squeezing from it a near-tragic, near-comic lyricism." Both Lefty and Pancho had found the blues to be the sheet music for their lives, having both experienced heartbreak and sorrow. For Pancho, it was that he had been an only child. He had had no one to build Christmas tree forts with, no one to teach him how to tip cows when they were asleep in some field, and no one to truly confide in about the messiness of some of his more "imaginative" dreams. For Lefty, it had been the long series of "incidents" that had hounded him from his earlier days. They had started with "the Astronaut Test incident," a common but rarely discussed event involving babysitters and their interests in a particular orifice. Then there was the "bowling ball incident," a deed so vile and too horrible to grasp even now that he was a man. There were others, but they were pushed back into a part of his brain that he rarely, if ever, revisited.

The key word there in the quote was "experience," as they had grown from these occurrences and become stronger because of them. To Lefty, that was the quintessence of this genre of music and maybe, just maybe, Bones was on to something when he would stare at the speaker during the crushing feedback of Hendrix's *Are You Experienced.*

Realizing they had been gone far too long, they retraced their steps and made it back to the shadows where they began to look for some wood to contribute to the fire. Finding only two small logs, they looked for the group in the near-darkness. Pancho got lucky and spotted them about fifty yards to the west and they gratefully picked up their pace.

As they neared the fire, Lefty froze in his tracks. He was able to make out the silhouette of the hated buccaneer with his cape flowing in the wind, casting long, supple shadows against a nearby parked car. He gestured grandly with the tricornered hat, to the delight of the girls, and Lefty began to see red. He screamed something that even he found impossible to translate and began to make his way to the camp. This caused the pirate to charge them at top speed with a strangely maniacal laugh. Lefty dropped his log and wondered what had become of Pancho. As the privateer closed the gap between them, Lefty realized he needed a weapon and surmised that the log would have to do, so he bent down and retrieved it with shaking hands. Perception had become reality as danger bore down on him like a diseased Cape buffalo. He deliberated about how quickly things had taken an evil and unrighteous turn.

Time slowed as Lefty visualized his gruesome death at the hands of this modern-day corsair. He remembered he had always planned on attending his own funeral, like Tom Sawyer, just not as the guest of honor. The murderer-to-be came to an abrupt stop ten yards short of his victim, raised both arms in the air, and howled a horrible laugh that stopped Lefty's heart. He closed his eyes in anticipation of the bloody extermination he faced and thought of home and how he wished he were there.

Just then, Pancho reached his side and yelled, "Is that you, Cal?"

When "Oh, yeah, baby!" rolled off Cal's tongue, Lefty felt the strength in his knees decide to take a vacation and he genuflected clumsily. He looked at the ground for a few moments and decided that it had been a good decision not to have eaten anything since the citrus this morning because he certainly would have involuntarily evacuated it about sixty seconds ago.

As the shock of it all subsided, Lefty rolled over on his back and enjoyed one of the most heartfelt belly laughs he could ever remember. Wiping away the tears of relief, he saw the girls descend on him, quickly followed by the caped lunatic who spread his costume over the lot of them, momentarily crushing out the last remaining air from Lefty's lungs. The gals grabbed the logs and returned to the encampment, followed by the Texans, who had a thousand questions for the interloper. Tequila was added to the last of the tea and then passed around the circle. Remembering the concert was still in full swing, the females lit out for a better look at the festivities, leaving the boys to catch up.

CHAPTER
TWENTY-ONE

As it turned out, Cal had fueled the plane with his super-petrol and followed them cross-country in case they needed a road man to guide them. *He* knew that his two pals had what it took to get through the trip, but did *they*? Would they become lost in their own souls, wandering through the godless landscape desperately cling-ing to the edge of sanity? Or would they conquer their demons and emerge with the knowledge and peace of mind that eludes the hardiest of men? Either way, he thought it would be best if he went along for the ride. He had followed them during their stay in Eden with as little contact as possible so that they might finish the journey on their own, but the girls had soon appeared and he, always having an eye for the ladies, could not help himself. The plane had been refueled and was parked at the airport, ready for a speedy getaway if needed. Cal filled in the other blanks for Lefty and Pancho while two new logs crackled in the Gogolian pyre.

As the band took a break to allow the extended percussion solos to veer out into space, the girls returned and the merry group once again danced around the fire to the beat of the drums. Cal had the pleasure of now having four young ladies trying to catch his eye and he delighted in the attention. Jilly whispered in Lefty's ear that she was glad he had not met his demise and clasped his hand anew. He could feel her breathe as they snuggled in the warmth of the now-dying flames, and they made wishes on shooting stars that were flying high above the low-clouded firmament.

Lefty awoke with a jolt as the music started again and then realized he had been in a dream state for an indeterminate amount of time. During this stretch, the wind had picked up and was blowing Jilly's fine hair across his face, tickling his nose and eyelashes. He tried to tickle her back, but seeing that he was awake, she jumped quickly away. He tried to catch her, doing some fire walking in the process, but she escaped his grasp. The others laughed when the soles of his boots began to smolder and he ran off through the sand to extinguish them. He returned with a shy look on his face after his heels had cooled, as it were, and rejoined the group with self-mockery. Jilly ran up and kissed him on the cheek, which was just the tonic he needed. It was decided that Cal and his four pirates-in-training would be the next to venture toward the music, and he strode energetically away, leading the pack looking more like a musketeer now that he had strapped a belt around his waist to keep the cape from taking flight and pulling him with it.

The original four found that the other girls had left their car unlocked, just as everyone in the Keys was apt to do, and discovered an ice chest under a blanket in the backseat. Lefty wished he had known about this when he found his footwear combusting, but he was glad to have a frosty adult beverage in his hand just the same. A jagged bolt of lightning about a mile offshore brought a gasp from the crowd and concern to the band as to whether the show would go on. Several quiet minutes later, the band started again as if nothing had happened, but it had been a harbinger of what was to come.

The wind continued to blow, but there appeared to be no rain forthcoming. The group crammed themselves on the trunk of the car and tried to watch the show. Soon, Jilly looked at Lefty with joyless eyes, as she had not anticipated Cal's arrival or their imminent departure in such a quick fashion.

"I just want you to know that if you ever make it back here one day, you have to *promise* me that you will give me a ring," Jilly said with her faraway eyes.

He found this confusing, and said, "Give you a ring? But...you *know* I'm married. She is a lot like you, though, and if I ever were to—"

"Stop it! Don't be an idgit. I meant give me a ring *on the phone.* When you *both* come back I promise to greet you at the gates to this kingdom of mine with open arms, and we all will play and laugh like we've done ever since I met you. If Dixie is anything like you, I'm sure that I will have made another true friend for life."

This flabbergasted him, and he once again lost his ability to speak. He felt the warmth of her hand in his as she leaned in close to kiss him, this time half on the mouth. She slapped her knees as she happily jumped off the trunk and said, "C'mon! We have a party to attend. I absolutely will not be maudlin on your last night here."

Lefty grabbed her rosy cheeks and kissed her lips hard. There was a lot of excitement in the air, as the ride was about to leave the platform again, probably for the last time, and all four adjusted their seat belts.

Now that the fire was out, it was decreed that the gang would leave the car and relocate as close to the stage as physically possible, even if it meant having to cram in with the masses. Upon hearing this, Jilly friskily agreed to do her part by squashing herself almost under Lefty's shirt. The plan was to attack from the rear by skirting the crowd and making their way back up the middle between the sound towers. This appeared to be a good strategy for two reasons. The first, and most important one, was that was where Cal and his crew had mentioned they would be. Second, coming from behind, you could see the stage while you were moving forward.

Cal stuck out like a sore thumb and was easy to find. Before their blitz into the crowd, the girls decided to find the public bathroom just a few hundred yards away, leaving the boys to compare notes and enjoy the insanity. Suddenly, there was a parting of the crowd just ahead of them, followed by screaming as a crazed man emerged from the crowd with his hand over his mouth. The three Texans stood like statues with vacant faces to watch this event. At the last possible moment, the lunatic veered toward them and lunged forward, his Technicolor vomit spewing between his fingers in distinct streams. Lefty and Pancho watched in horror as this geyser erupted between and on either side of them where they stood frozen in the sand. Cal was not so fortunate. He had taken a direct hit in the face and stood there with an expression of disbelief. The kid who had experienced this "reversal of fortune" had run off and, upon regaining his senses, Cal ran after him, screaming at the top of his lungs. He soon caught him and jumped on him bareback like a rodeo bronco. The two rode away, disappearing into the darkness, with Cal flailing at the cad the entire time. It was several moments before Pancho broke out in a gut-busting laugh, causing Lefty to follow suit. They were still snorting hard when the girls returned, so the boys tried to retell the tale without throwing up themselves from the hilarity of it all.

Cal returned about twenty minutes later, minus his cape and hat and soaking wet. Not getting any relief from waling on the spurting perpetrator, he had run into the surf at full speed, shoes and all. Luckily, he had four young ladies to mother him and was soon laughing at his misfortune. His attendants began to lick him dry like cats, with the wind doing most of the work. He looked at Lefty and Pancho, now wondering just who the unlucky ones were. He flashed his canines as he cackled in delight, upping the volume when one of the girls began to chew on his erect finger like an ear of sweet Nebraska corn.

As the group was preparing to move closer to the stage and away from the lunatic fringe along the periphery, a lone bolt of lightning shot across the sky which momentarily caused the stage lights to flicker. The music never stopped, although it did cause some of the less resilient concertgoers to pack up their gear and start toward town, back to the relative safety of a Duval Street bar. This eased the approach to the stage and they soon found a pleasant spot up close. The band seemed to be building toward a finale, not only for the safety of the crowd, but for their own.

From the side of the dais, Lefty observed a familiar female figure appear on stage and make her way toward the band. *Holy shit. It's her,* Lefty thought. A spotlight soon found her form and lit her in a bath of blue radiance. Lefty immediately recognized the wizard's hat as being the one he had seen at Danton and Mickey's party. The music slowly faded away as the band saw the bold con-jurer approach them, and stopped altogether when she raised her wand in defiance of the storm. With a flick of her magic stick, sparks shot out over the crowd and slowly cascaded back to earth in slow motion before twinkling out. With her free hand, she threw a fireball to the sky, and the crowd watched silently as it sailed through the low clouds and disappeared. She continued to throw these meteoroids around and several exploded over the crowd's heads. Lefty noticed that Jilly's grip on his hand had become increasingly more like a vise and his blood flow had become restricted. He felt it pulse through his veins with a loud *thump... thump...thump* and he started to panic. Where was the beating coming from? Was it all in his head, or was his heart about to explode? With fear in his eyes, he looked to see that Jilly's jaw had unknow-ingly become unhinged and she looked strangely grotesque in the fiery light. The look of wonder on her face as she gazed skyward explained a lot and he gently tried to help her close her gaping mouth. Working with both hands, she was finally able to pop the bone back into place, and once again regained her loveliness.

Pancho, having the better eyesight of the two, yelled in Lefty's ear that it was the very same wizard from the full moon party. Looking closer, he agreed that she looked the same, but how could that be? Before he had had time to finish the thought, the wizard pointed the wand in his general direction and shot a comet of fire that caught him square on his jaw, knocking him to the ground. The crowd gasped as his friends, both old and new, helped him back to his feet. Jilly tried to wipe away a scorch mark she found on the tip of his nose and then pulled his face into her chest. At any other given time in his life, this would have had him in seventh heaven, but pres-ently he wasn't even sure if he was alive at all.

A blinding bolt of lightning brought him and the crowd back to life. The thunderclap that followed shortly thereafter heralded the end of the show and large, meaty drops of rain began to fall. Like the Bard had written, you don't need a weatherman to know which way the wind blows, so the tea party confederacy helped Lefty move off the beach and back to the car.

When they arrived, Cal stated, "I think the time has come, my friends. It's time to fly the friendly skies of AirCal. Let's get to the airport before they shutter the joint up."

Lefty wasn't about to leave the items in the locker at the bus depot, and shouted, "Not a chance! I've got to have my notes. This whole trip would be for shit if I don't have them! Besides, there's tequila for the flight home."

This caught Cal's attention. "Alright, then. You and Jilly make a ball's-out run for the roses and meet us back at the airport. Here, let me drive," he said to the prettiest of his new clique, adding with his canine snarl, "I need to keep my hands busy or I might be looking at a Mann Act charge."

Jilly drove her friend's car cautiously on the slick streets as the rain began to blow sideways. Lefty admired her concentration and delicately placed his hand on her shoulder. She tucked her chin down to nuzzle his hand, only to have her jaw unhinge once again. She pulled over and quickly worked it back into its socket. At the depot, Lefty hurriedly opened the locker, retrieved his scant belongings, and jumped back in the passenger seat. The rain slowed to a drizzle as the car wound its way to the empty airport. Cal was inside begging for clearance as the two arrived on the tarmac and ran to the small plane. Pancho was on the brink of not getting on the plane at all and making a go of it in paradise. Evidently, there had been some conversation on this subject with Connie and he had become extremely torn between his two alternatives. He was privately hoping that they would not be able to leave tonight at all and his decision would have been made for him. When Cal returned with the news that the airport was now officially closing and theirs would be the last plane out, his options had run their course. He and Connie said their good-byes away from prying eyes behind the fuselage of the plane. A lost pair of panties and a bra found their sanctuary on the damp concrete.

Cal started the engines and yelled that it was time to take off. Lefty waved farewell to his new partners in crime, and watched as Jilly slowly walked up to him and put her arms around his neck. He prepared for a kiss and wiped the rain from his face. She dropped one of her arms and handed him the present she had been conceal-ing for the last several hours. It was a piece of scrimshaw that her best friend had given to her for luck and she wanted it to go to Dixie. She said she seemed to already be lucky enough having met him and that she probably wouldn't need it anymore. She said that Dixie was already lucky, too. She winked at him with a smile before hug-ging him again. There would be no long good-byes here, and as she turned and danced between the raindrops back to the car, she yelled, "We'll always have Paris!"

Lefty climbed aboard and sat in the back. Smiling, he looked at the ornate piece of ivory and ran its smoothness across his cheek. With a thud, Pancho landed in the front seat, zipped up his fly and closed the door. Cal taxied the plane away as the girls waved from inside the sedan. Then, one of the wilder ones mooned them and everyone laughed.

As they gained speed on the runway, Cal said that he had had a fine time. The other two could only nod in agreement as the wheels left the ground and the lights of Key West began to glow from below. Sixty seconds later, they broke through the clouds to the blinding light of a perfectly full moon, and Lefty decided then and there that they were indeed in heaven.

As he tried to recollect the events of the past few days, he was astounded to comprehend the vastness of his spiritual being. He had crossed over the old high-water marks of his soul and discovered new boundaries that were further out there than even he had ever expected to find. He had gone to the desert and confronted, then befriended, the serpent. He had followed the tunnel to the white light and found that it was not of death at all, but of life itself. In quiet desperation, he had learned that he had been born a long way from where he needed to be, and found that the long road home was not always well traveled. The filters to his programmed brain had been lifted away and new vistas had become part of his novel landscape. Had he gone all the way? Had he been out to where the air was thin?

Noting that his glorious absence from account-ability was coming to an end, his thoughts returned to Key West and what lay ahead for its denizens. This storm would pass it by like so many others had before, but not before it got a good douching to cleanse away the hedonistic filth, leaving in its wake a greener utopia for at least a day or two. The return to "normalcy" would find people crawling out of their hiding places and retak-ing their bohemian home. Ancient toothless men would once again dance in the backstreets after helping the angry Negro youth sweep away the sin and debris. Birds would return in time and the isle would begin life again. He beamed as he remembered the words Jilly had spoken at the groggery before the show and knew he would probably take her up on her advice. He would return sometime, not as a warrior tourist, but as an enthusiast—of life.

Lefty remembered a quote from Mark Twain that his mother had read to him many times as a child, and found that it now had a new, special meaning to him:

> *Twenty years from now you will be more disappointed*
> *by the things that you didn't do*
> *than by the ones you did do.*
> *Sail away from the safe harbor.*
> *Catch the trade winds in your sails.*
> *Explore. Dream. Discover.*

He looked over at Pancho and thought he saw a tear roll down his sunburned face. Lefty then put his head against the cool window and, with a warm smile on his face, quietly closed his tired eyes and swam to the moon. Long time gone, indeed...

CHAPTER
TWENTY-TWO

Austin, Texas

In unison, Lefty and Pancho broke the surface of the cold spring waters and swam to the nearest ladder. They wrenched themselves up and tried to quell the shivers that covered them from head to toe. Both had bluish lips that seemed to be quite numb. When they were finally able to make it back to their spot, the towels and backpack were intact and appeared untouched. This was all very confusing and they looked around in a disoriented state. How did they get back to Austin? Did they ever leave at all? Was it all a surreal dream that had now left them tremulous and disbelieving? Or had it been a cerebral and spiritual voyage to the edge of reason that had eluded so many others through time? Had they finally rid their garden of evil? They had shared certain visions that held value to their beliefs and dogma. It was as if Lefty had finally been fitted with the proper pair of glasses, and with these, the crispness and translucency of his world was now forever changed. For good or ill, he knew things would be different from now on. That much was for sure.

His mind was flying again and he wanted to get off the roller coaster. He turned to look at Pancho and could see that the glaze in his eyes was most likely the mirror-image of his own. He watched as Pancho's pupils darted around their environs, never staying put for more than a split second. He eventually blinked and then abruptly turned to Lefty. He had an economy of words for the moment, but his eyes said what his tongue could not. Disbelief filled his spirit, as it was entirely Herculean to process the events of the last...what? Hours? Days?

Lefty called on the things that they enjoyed most to pull them together and get them going. Food and music were the therapeutic agents needed and he knew where to find them. Pancho eagerly nodded in agreement and they collected their belongings. The pool was closing, and the knowing look from a lifeguard on their way out acknowledged that they had indeed had a por-tentous and singular day in the life of two travel-ers. Like so many of the other employees of the pool, the lifeguard had traveled many a mile in their boots and recognized the familiar dazed and confused look. He smiled broadly as they exited the turnstile and wished them well.

The large parking lot was deserted as they made their way up the tree-lined drive. A breeze carried the scent of freshly mown grass, and the first cicadas of the year used their acoustic talents to perform the symphony so familiar to natives of central Texas in the summertime. A few short blocks away was Chuy's. The dirt parking lot disguised the uniqueness of the interior and the flavor of the food. Lefty had long ago decided that it did not matter how dirty the floor was if the ceiling was as enchanting as this cantina's. There seemed to be a thousand fish floating above the bar area, suspended in air and always moving. The walls were filled with everything Elvis. And then there were the hubcaps. They were nailed to anything that would hold them and all shared a peculiar rustiness found only on old automobile accessories. Some enterprising young man must have attended a Mexican demolition derby, bought the entire inventory that was left over, and brought it back stateside.

They were able to find a booth quickly and were soon brought fresh corn tortillas, butter, and a large bowl of piquant salsa that was brimming with cilantro and onion. A smaller, separate bowl of jalape os was placed near the in-booth jukebox with a warning that they were "nuclear." Lefty had never met a pepper he didn't like, but this caution made him pause. Pancho inhaled an entire pepper in one bite while Lefty looked for signs of discomfort. A belch of approval without the need of some form of liquid coolant acquiesced Lefty's reservations and he happily bit one in half. The waitress had arrived with two incredibly large tumblers of water just in time to witness Lefty's head exploding and the resulting tears that followed. As Lefty was unable to speak, although this time for a very different reason, Pancho took over the ordering process.

"Hmmm, let's see what we have here...I think they *all* sound good. I think we'll need to have one of everything on the left side over here for starters," he said efficiently, "and, hmmm...Left, you got a lot of that bankroll left, don't you? Nice. So, let's try everything over here on the right side, too. Except for that mole, it gives me some horrible gas and we don't need any more of that. Now, as for the libations...bring us two of your *very* strongest top-shelf margaritas, extra salt. *Each*." Pancho folded the menu and sat back as if this was an everyday occurrence, which with him it was.

Lefty was in no shape to contradict the amount ordered and had to be comforted by the fact that it was a rather small menu. As the pain from the capsaicin subsided, Lefty wiped the tears from his eyes and began to examine the miniature jukebox that was in every booth. He found almost every Elvis record ever made and then spied something that made him cringe. "Time in a Bottle" by Jim Croce stared back at him, and he thought that if the jukebox in heaven had this song, he would opt for warmer climes down under. Luckily, the beverages arrived and Elvis was in command of the playlist.

With familiar surroundings once again in their sights, Lefty relaxed and tried to replay in his mind the recent events that had occurred. He carefully reached into the backpack and retrieved the diary that had lodged under the half-empty bottle of mescal. The binding had a light coating of a silica-type material that stuck to Lefty's fingertips. He swirled it between his thumb and forefinger before placing it on his lips. It had no distinguishable taste, was inconsistent in its makeup, and appeared to be sand. He opened the log to the first page and saw something he had never expected to see. There was a beautiful white page before him that held no words. He hurriedly flipped through the remaining pages with the same result, finding only clean, crisp, empty pages. Crestfallen, he looked to Pancho for empathy, and finding none, slowly closed the barren tome. This was more than disheartening and left him mouthing the words, "What happened?"

Pancho reached across the tortillas and snatched the diary from his grasp. Ever the more sensible one, Pancho reasoned that it was some form of invisible ink that Lefty had subconsciously used to prevent these important documents from falling into the wrong, uninitiated hands. He sat back very satisfied with his interpretation and cracked his knuckles. Neither of them was in any kind of shape to realize that the pen had never worked in the first place.

Thankfully, the food arrived, with the help of two waiters and a somewhat disgruntled dishwasher who had been enlisted in the delivery of this massive order. Lefty almost felt a bit embarrassed by the sheer quantity of the repast, but was eager to sample the fare immediately. Pancho promptly took charge of the distribution of the different dishes with the zeal of an auctioneer and the precision and polish of a skilled surgeon. These two friends had eaten so many meals together that it was basically an unwritten fiat that Pancho would taste everything before it was passed, and Lefty was comfortable with the procedure. He accepted this because if Pancho did not like it, it was inevitable he wouldn't, either. After all, it was Pancho who had taught him that Chinese food was not chicken chow mein in a can with fried noodles in the top compartment. He had also taught him that Italian cuisine wasn't just pizza, and that there was a major distinction between northern and southern recipes.

Despite the size of their order, most of it was consumed rapidly. Pancho wiped his lips with the red cloth napkin that had been replaced more than once since the feast had begun and leaned back in the high-backed wooden chair.

"Lefty, I might be able to squeeze in one last thing before we move to the bar, and I was thinking about a large order of *queso flameado.* What do you think? You don't 'bind' easily, do you?"

Lefty responded, "Uhhh, Pancho, I don't know if an order of flaming cheese might be the most flawless choice considering the amount of high-octane alcohol that remains on the table. Now, if we wanted to hire a busboy to stand over us with a fire extinguisher, I might be persuaded to take a sniff. I like cheese, but nah, I'm too full. Don't even think about it. You're still a fool even after all we have been through."

The two motioned to the server and announced that they would be moving to the bar. She carried their drinks to the cantina and placed the bill on the bar top, complete with two "come-back" mints.

"I'll be getting off here shortly, so when you are ready, just pay at the register," the waitress said as she was walking away.

"Whoa! Hang on there, little lady," Pancho blurted out between belches of refried beans. "Don't you think you deserve a tip this evening? With what we put you through, you might need to see a chiropractor. Do you have change for his fifty?" he added, pointing to Secretary of the Exchequer, Lefty. "No, I think you deserve the whole thing. Lefty, be so kind as to hand her that bill and tell her to keep the change. Go ahead."

Lefty wasn't quite sure how this had become his burden, but he did it cheerfully, anyway.

Her name was Kat, and she turned out to be quite the conversationalist who laughed at all their stories. She wasn't sure about what to make of their "journey," but seemed to understand a bit more and showed real interest when the Grateful Dead was mentioned. She had been to many shows over the years, even spending an entire summer on the road following them across the country. Since the talk had turned to music, Kat wondered if the pair was going to the show tonight at the Armadillo World Headquarters. A kid from Jersey who was making quite a name for himself was in town and had been to the restaurant earlier that day. As a tip, the band had left her some passes to the concert. She had appreciated this, as they were a scruffy bunch and could barely afford the meal, much less a cash tip. She was fine with that. She said his name was Bruce and that he had possessed a wonderful, high laugh that seemed to contradict his deep voice. She had never heard of him before, but the tickets were free and the auditorium was just down the street. Lefty was thinking it was time to get back home and was going to beg off, when Pancho decided for both of them that they could not possibly miss it. He had heard of this guy and his particularly energetic shows that would sometimes go on for more than three hours. Lefty remembered he had signed up for the entire journey, not just the first leg, and quickly decided to follow Pancho's lead. He had led Lefty in the right musical direction many times in the past, so this was no time to second-guess the proposal. After the tab was paid, he felt energized by the food, drink, and camaraderie once again, and they made their way to the door.

CHAPTER
TWENTY-THREE

Kat had an ancient Volkswagen bus parked around back that reeked of patchouli and strange tobacco. It took several minutes before the engine finally turned over and they lurched out onto the street, which violently threw the occupants around inside the vehicle. While Lefty looked for a seat belt, Kat was hunched over the steering column, her fingers in a death grip on the wheel, driving like a woman possessed. She chattered animatedly while she drove, lit a cigarette, tuned the radio, and shifted gears simultaneously, and Lefty felt an accident was imminent. Pancho was singing at the top of his lungs from the backseat and seemed not to have noticed this seventh, and final, sign of the apocalypse that was unfolding before their eyes, as Kat wove through traffic and took corners like a NASCAR veteran on amphetamines with several warrants out for "excessive speed."

Outside her home, she came to an abrupt stop which threw Lefty against the dash with such force it seemed to have loosened his money-teeth substantially. Horrified at the thought of early dentures, he examined each tooth carefully, before concluding that the damage was minimal. Meanwhile, Kat had disappeared into the house that she shared with three roommates to change out of her work clothes. This brought about the end of Pancho's singing as he publicized his intent to enter the house in the hope of catching the roomies in a pillow fight. Privately, Lefty hoped to encounter something a little more substantial, like possibly a lingerie tickle fight, and hurriedly followed his pal in through the front door.

They were both disenchanted to find a living room full of fully clad males and two yapping dogs. Uncomfortable small talk was made between the dwellers and the intruders while Kat finished her metamorphosis into a fine-looking young concertgoer. She returned to the large front room, noted the time, and said that they should depart shortly. Lefty noticed his palms begin to sweat at the thought of another death-ride, but reminded himself that what didn't kill him would make him stronger. He thought about the absurdity of that notion as he frantically searched for the seat belt and then hitched it tight. Digging his boot heels into the threadbare material that once passed for carpeting, he grabbed for the mescal with one hand and the door handle with the other, just in case he might have to eject himself when the bus erupted in a giant ball of fire. He needn't have worried, as Kat was too busy rolling some joints for her to defy the laws of physics to any great degree. He tilted the bottle up to his lips and watched as the worm floated downward to his tongue. He carefully sucked it into his gullet and swallowed it whole.

The pickled worm in a bottle of mescal was famously known to bring on fantastic visions when ingested, and Lefty thought the time was right. He wiped his lips with the sleeve of his shirt and passed the remains to the backseat. With gusto, Pancho slurped down the last of it, discharged another malodorous "refried" belch, and grinned as they pulled into the world-famous Armadillo. The sign out front simply read: "SPRINGSTEEN."

Perhaps the Armadillo might never have existed if not for the demise of the Vulcan Gas Company. The Vulcan was the only mid-size venue for the burgeoning Austin music scene until it closed its doors in late 1969. A month later, the Armadillo made its debut and quickly took over as the pre-eminent concert hall in the Southwest. The music was a unique mix of rock, country, redneck rock, blues, psychedelia, Tejano, and folk, all thrown into a blender and turned on to frappé. This made for unusual artist pairings and, with that, unusual audiences. One night, there might be Quicksilver Messenger Service opening for bluesman Freddie King, and the next, Indian sitarist Ravi Shankar and Jerry Jeff Walker. This halcyon environment proved to be a fertile locale for new acts, estab-lished acts, and even groups that easily could have sold out stadiums, all because of the aura that the Armadillo held in its hippie/redneck fist.

The arena, if it could be called that, was located in an old National Guard armory in south Austin off Barton Springs Road, behind a skating rink and George's Cactus Club. It was hard to find if you didn't know where to look, but was worth the trouble to seek it out. Kat was obviously a Dillo veteran and skillfully maneuvered the venerable bus into the tightly packed lot. Flashing her passes and a peace sign to the lone, long-haired attendant, she was somehow able to secure a spot almost alongside the building itself. After another puff or two, she blithely threw the butt into the overstuffed ashtray and announced their departure. Lefty eyed the ember that still seemed to be lit and crushed it out on the ground with his boot. He thought it would be prudent not to return to a burned-out shell of the old vehicle in case they needed another quick getaway. She handed him a new cigarette and asked him to put it in his shirt pocket "just in case."

They proceeded straight to the beer garden, where they purchased three two-dollar pitchers of cold Shiner beer and found an empty picnic table. There were smiles everywhere, and a dense cloud of blue smoke seemed to hang under the large oak trees that canopied the garden. Amazingly, Lefty found a familiar face through that cloud and vaulted out of his seat. He grabbed his cousin Lou and hugged her tightly. It had been ages since they had been in contact, but as it always is between two friends, they quickly caught up with the comings and goings of old companions and family and exchanged phone numbers, with her promising to take him out to the lake house in the coming week for a day on the water. She made world-class margaritas and had let her secret recipe slip away late one night around a comfortable campfire next to the lake. Her mantra was, "Always use fresh key limes, two dashes of orange juice, and sea salt instead of kosher to rim the glass." She had sworn him to secrecy and he had never betrayed her trust. Secret smiles were traded as they held hands for a moment and then kissed, just before she danced away with a wave of her well-manicured nails. He wiped the lipstick from his cheek and found his way back to the table. Things were going nicely for Lefty and he appreciated being able to see her, even for such a short period of time. *Another true friend with which to share the journey,* he thought. *And one who appreciates the value of a good key lime... what else might happen tonight?*

Alvin Crow and the Pleasant Valley Boys were just finishing up their set with the crowd favorite, "Nyquil Blues," and so the three friends had probably thirty minutes to make their way to the balcony before the main act from Jersey took the stage. They each took turns finding the bathroom while the others held the table. This took longer than expected, as the restrooms, particularly the men's, were jammed with people making transactions of various kinds. There seemed to be some type of countercultural economy that existed here, somewhat like the open markets of Paris that sold goods and services to the local bourgeoisie from stalls in the town square. There were stalls here alright, but these had urine puddles underfoot instead of straw. Lefty surmised from the amount of aspirin being sold tonight that there must be a lot of headaches going around. Someone shouted that he was in need of "disco biscuits" and this confused most of the crowd. Everyone in Texas knew what biscuits were, but what was a "disco"? Lefty shrugged and continued on his mission to make it to a urinal before there was an accident. After he found the needed receptacle, he rejoined the others just as a clamorous applause erupted from inside the hall. They hurriedly found the darkened stairs and once again climbed on board.

Leaving the bathroom, Lefty had begun to notice that things were...well, a little different. People seemed to be moving a little slower, their movements a little more robotic, and trails seemed to follow any noticeable changes of position. He could see where people had been just seconds before, just like machines in the old penny arcades where cards flashed by to create a moving pic-ture. He wondered what was causing all these people to behave so strangely, until he reached the top of the stairs and entered the openness of the cavernous space. Spotlights and colored stage lights were replicating the slurred motion he had witnessed just moments before, and then it hit him. Time was actually slowing down for him to enjoy this event to its fullest!

He harked back to all the good deeds he had done in his life and was curious which wonderful and illustrious act it was that afforded him this gift. Was it that he had paid all his library fines since the fifth grade? Until recently, he had always eaten fish on Fridays, even though he wasn't Catholic. He had never torn the tags off any pillow he had ever owned and, most importantly, he had always observed warning signs, mostly because it was a state law. One most certainly had to follow all laws, even the particularly absurd state ones. Or could it have been the time he didn't talk to the nice man at the park who offered him candy?

These thoughts were interrupted by a sharp smack to his forehead, courtesy of Pancho. More dazed than hurt, only then did Lefty realize that he had drool running from the corners of his mouth that had fallen to the floor and formed a small puddle. He was now a huge distraction to his friends from the show that was unfolding on the stage. Handing him a handkerchief, Pancho threw back his head and laughed manically. He had been in the same frame of mind just an instant before and beat his friend to the punch, as it were. They were definitely on a different plane, now that the worm (in Lefty's case) and mescal had worked its way from their stomachs to their minds, and they were ready for anything.

The concert turned out to be almost a religious experience. There were songs where the entire crowd danced wildly and others that had them weeping like children. Encore after encore left the audience hoarse but needing more from this unknown deacon of rock and roll. The finale to the sermon brought the audience to a frenzied crescendo and then crashed unexpectedly to a halt. The lights went out for several minutes, giving the crowd time to catch their collective breath before the houselights came on with a strangely white, sterile truth. Everything seemed institutionalized by the overly bright beams that filled Lefty's eyes, not unlike the dentist's office after a particularly long procedure that most probably involved X-rays and painkillers that ended in the suffix "-caine."

Now that he thought about it, he did appear to be numb, not from any sociopathic dentist, but from the music that rang in his ears. It had been heavenly and left him stunned. He watched the crowd file out with sweat and shock on their faces before he turned to his friends. They both had glowing looks of wonderment, as if they had just been witness to a spiritual healing on a grand scale. Wordlessly, they turned and joined the throng of new disciples that were filing down the stairwell.

The beer garden was still open and was just the oasis needed to regain their faculties. Beers were obtained, along with some unusual ginseng drinks that Lefty found delicious. He switched his empty cup for Pancho's full one when his back was turned to watch a curious girl in a flowing dress covered in brilliant sunbursts and reddish quasars. She had been sitting at the end of their table unnoticed until now, and appeared to be sucking on a strand of light blue rings. Pancho looked closer and discovered that she was actually biting them off and chewing them.

"I couldn't help but notice that you are eating that fine jewelry of yours. Is there something wrong, something that I might be able to help you with? And just what is that, exactly?" Pancho asked gently.

"Oh, it's a necklace my boyfriend gave me as a going-away present. He's leaving me for another guy, of all things. I guess that doesn't say much for me as a lover, huh? He designed it all by himself and it's made of Valium, I think. He said I might need it. To get over his leaving, I mean."

This certainly explained the vacant, faraway eyes, so Pancho put on his best doctor's hat and tried to explain to her that it was time to find a friend to drive her home. "Where are your friends that you came with, hon? I think you might need somebody to look after you if you keep on eating those tranquilizers like that."

"I don't really have too many friends, not like you have," she said blankly. "Do you think you might be able to give me a lift? I don't live real far from here."

Pancho was beginning to worry that he might have a nutcase on his hands, and helplessly looked around for Lefty to come to the rescue. After awhile, Kat agreed to give the poor child a ride and they all sat once again at the picnic table.

After the drinks were finished and Pancho gave up trying to figure out what had happened to his ginseng, this new gang of four found the bus intact and was ready to roll. The waif had resumed gnawing on her necklace, so Pancho asked her if the others might admire it up close. This old "out of sight, out of mind" ruse worked to perfection, and she soon had forgotten all about her pharmaceutical jewelry. Pancho crunched several of the aquamarine pearls off the string, which left his brilliant teeth a bit discolored, before carefully placing the strand in the watch pocket of his Wranglers.

Lefty asked if they could possibly run by the campus because he had something he wanted Pancho's advice on. The merry group journeyed up Lamar, passing by the darkened homes of the local gentry who were safely tucked abed in their Tarrytown towers. They easily found their way to campus, which at this time of night was serene and unlearned, and parked the bus near the library. The boys left Kat to keep an eye on their new patient and walked to the front of one of the largest buildings on campus. They found a place to sit on the low wall facing this edifice, knowing that within a few short hours this promenade would be brimming with the future leaders of this and other communities.

Lefty looked to his right and recognized a familiar building. It was a place he had become quite intimate with when he was a student at the university and was home to the school's supercomputer. It took up almost an entire floor but was a remarkable machine. Lefty would spend countless hours punching holes in "computer cards" that, when assimilated in the proper order, could solve various math computations like $(8 + 4) \times 2 = 24$. If it wasn't for those pesky hours spent punching the holes, it made for a fine calculator. The sheer weight of the cards alone was enough to give someone a hernia, and the constant lugging of them back and forth from house to class made it a chore. He finally decided to give up on this computer business entirely and fell back on his keen knowledge of his handy slide rule.

They sat quietly and stared at the brightly lit facade. After a moment, Lefty looked up at his best friend, then back to the edifice and asked, "Well, do you think we are experienced now?"

Pancho looked up at the star-filled sky and scratched the back of his head with his considerable fingernails. He then slowly rubbed his reddened eyes and let out a meager sigh. After looking at the script sculpted into the structure once again, he threw a familiar paw over Lefty's shoulder, saying, "I just don't know yet. Let's talk about it later." He winked at his friend and tried to stand on unsteady feet, saying, "I think it is that time, my friend...time to board that bus for the last part of the journey. We're almost there. It has been one hell of a trip, I can assure you that. Got kind of wild there for a spell, but as always, we survived. And I certainly couldn't have done it without you by my side. It was just meant to be, that's all. Now I need to get laid something fierce. All that fine tail at the show got me jazzed up again and I just have to spill some seed right about now. I think that goes without saying."

He started to turn and walk back to the bus, but not before he saw Lefty slowly shake his head in disagreement, hoping his longtime friend would understand. He needed to get back, back to his family and the things he loved. There had been enough of the unknown for now and he would savor the familiarity of his home. They both knew that spring would come again.

Pancho rose and hugged his friend, and then, with a wave, he was gone. Lefty softly called after him, "You know where the key is," not knowing if Pancho had even heard.

He lowered himself down and sat on the ground using the wall to prop up his weary back. He again looked up at the sentence etched into the stone that he had seen every day for years. "And ye shall know the truth, and the truth shall make you free."

He didn't think he had necessarily been freed, just...well, maybe it would be better to think about it later. He got to his feet, shook off as much dust as he could, and set off to finish the rest of his journey.

CHAPTER
TWENTY-FOUR

As Lefty turned the last corner to his house, his spirit was filled with a sense of profound growth and spiritual wellness. It felt like he had rubbed sunshine all over his now brown face. For some reason, the street was dimmer this night, dimmer than most, and Lefty wondered if he had sapped all the electricity from his neighborhood. But the sidewalk knew his footsteps and led him to his home straightaway. The dogs of his neighborhood seemed to have lost their bark for the night and were curled up on their porches. A few lifted their heads before returning to dream the dreams of dogs. Dogs, like most animals, can smell fear. And after this adventure, there wasn't much fear left in Lefty. Two houses down, Lefty spotted the flag that was whipping in the breeze over Cal's house. As he got closer, he saw that it was a new banner, one that he could only laugh about now. It was a skull and crossbones and he stopped to admire it for several minutes. Perhaps this really hadn't been a dream after all. It might have happened just the way they remembered it. But what about the journal? Why hadn't the pen done its part to capture the sights, smells, and visions in this, their most important, journey?

As he moved past Cal's house, he saw a sight that made him smile. For hundreds of years, sailors returning home from their seafaring adventures eagerly looked for a candle burning in the window to welcome them back. In his large bay window, a small, dim flicker of light radiated from what was formerly a twelve-inch pillar candle. It had become a puddle of red tallow, and as the wick finally gasped its last breath, it drowned just as he walked up the drive. As he neared the steps to the house, he froze on the gravel. Atop those steps were two black figures, still as statues. After what seemed like ages, Pinkie mewed while Bones wondered aloud, "Where have you been all this time?" Visibly relieved that this was not an assault from another wave of electricity or an angry badger, he made himself comfortable on the second step from the top so they might have an eye-to-eye conversation. He was greeted warmly and they informed him of all the activities that had happened to them in his absence.

Lefty reached in the upper pocket on the inside of his jacket and produced the cigarette procured at the Armadillo. With a quick stroke, he lit it and leaned back to relive the adventures in his head. The light from the two-inch kitchen match illuminated a present Pinkie had for him that Lefty hadn't noticed before. Under her right paw was a mouse about the size of a small beefsteak tomato. It was wounded, not dead, for when Pinkie lifted her paw to present the gift, the mouse was able to limp away. The match burned Lefty's thumb and forefinger and he cursed, tossing the charred stick into the daffodils. As he fumbled for another, there seemed to be some sort of skirmish to his left. As the would-be torch lit the night and cast dancing shadows once again around the porch, Lefty saw an amazing sight. The head of the mouse had disappeared into Pinkie's mouth. The rest of the body struggled as it dangled from her lips. The screams of the rodent were muffled, and for that Lefty was thankful. He had experienced enough blood and violence inside his head lately. Inch by inch, it began to disappear down her throat, much like the constrictors of South America downing a paca. He found it impossible that her thin throat could accommodate this rodent, and eventually all that was left was the long tail hanging from her lips.

She looked at Lefty proudly. She now had a serpentine tongue that twitched in a circle like a whirligig. He was worried that she would not be able to breathe, because her larynx was clearly blocked. She crouched down and curled her paws underneath herself until she looked like the meatloaf his mother made for him in his youth on special occasions. With an audible slurp, the tail disappeared forever. Lefty swore he heard a small belch being emitted from her petite mouth shortly afterward.

This sequence was of much interest to him. He had had cats in his household since he was in big boy pants and had never seen this act performed in front of him. It seemed perfectly natural for a cat to catch a mouse and eat it, but like Pancho's crying, he had never witnessed it before. Nature had come full circle and he was there to admire it. Darwin had gotten it right after all, and now Lefty had become his newest disciple. Survival of the fittest, indeed.

With thoughts of strange, faraway places bubbling up in his frazzled cranium, he thoughtfully stroked his beard. Bones cocked his head, much the way a dog does when it hears a noise it hasn't heard before, and looked at him quizzically. He blurted out something about the now two-inch gray beard he sported. Lefty was astonished. How long had he been gone? Had this sacrament just sped up the aging process even if only minutely? He certainly felt wiser, more insightful, and more perceptive of the world around him. If he could only apply this newfound knowledge intelligently, he might find out that he had not hit the high-water mark. There might be more out there in the ether waiting to be gleaned by him, bit by bit. Thinking that he was probably repeating thoughts over and over to himself, he shrugged his shoulders and tried not to make too much of it at this juncture.

Exhausted, Lefty stood and stretched his long, bone-weary legs. He tried once again to shake off as much of the dust and decadence from his jeans and boots as he could, but to no avail. He silently pulled the boots off and placed them by the front door. No need to start tomorrow off with grumblings of a dusty house. He hugged the kids and opened the large front door. He turned to see the cats split up, with Pinkie darting across the freshly mown lawn and Bones just squeezing in the door as it closed. He watched through the open bay window as Pinkie carefully crossed the darkened street and leaped upon Townes's porch. She turned and sat down, looking much like an empress on her throne. She gazed up the street and then back down, surveying her imaginary troops. All seemed to be well in her kingdom.

Bones followed Lefty into the library and curled up beneath the wooden speakers. *This isn't the time for Hendrix, you big toad*, thought Lefty. He sat at his rolltop desk, lifted the handle, and the slatted cover disappeared inside itself. He pulled out a fresh pad and carefully sharpened three No. 2 pencils with his whittling knife. There would be no more ink involved with anything relating to the voyage from now on. He chose the longest of the three leaded points and wrote in large block letters: "INTO THE MYSTIC."

He now had two choices: he could begin to write while these images, both blissful and horrific, were still fresh in his mind, or he could clamber up the stairs to his sanctuary. He reluctantly chose the latter and rose to douse the candles that his muse had left burning for him in the hall. He left the desk open and made his way upstairs with Bones at his heels. He quietly opened the door and slid inside. He carefully folded his jeans and placed them in the wicker hamper inside the cedar closet. His socks and shirt soon followed, and he turned to survey the room. As was her wont, everything was in its place and fresh gardenias perfumed the entire second floor. The combination of the cedar and the blooms made for a delicious and comforting fragrance, disguising the road stench that had become Lefty's shadow. The antique four-poster bed looked even more inviting than usual. With a feather mattress, down comforter, and six eiderdown pillows, this was truly a bed built for sleep. The freshly ironed Egyptian cotton sheets were the icing on the cake.

Bones sat at the foot of the bed and looked intently at the spot atop the bed he hoped to land upon. In a split second, he was on the bed, dangling belly and all. He curled up at Dixie's feet and fell asleep immediately. Lefty slipped under the covers with as little movement as possible. He looked at Dixie's peaceful smile and wondered how he had gotten so lucky.

She slowly opened her eyes. She wasn't the least bit startled to have a bearded man in her bed. And after a moment, she said with a giggle, "I see that the bail fund didn't have to come into play. I'm just really glad you are back and all in one piece. You just never know what might happen when Pancho's involved. I swear, you two get into more trouble... Did you have some of the barbecue I left out for you? Danton dropped it off thinking you might need some comfort food when you guys got back. And just where is Pancho anyway? Is he already asleep?"

Lefty scratched his neck and said quietly, "No, ma'am. He's still out there chasing rainbows. Just as well...I probably wouldn't ever get to sleep with him jabbering on about our adventure. Sometimes, you just have to put on the brakes and rest a bit. At least that's the way I see it tonight. I saw the barbecue and I just knew it was from old Danton. He knows how to smoke some meat, alright. I thought I'd save it for lunch tomorrow. I'll probably appreciate it more then. Besides, you should have seen the meal we had tonight. Just when I thought I'd seen it all..."

Lefty's tired voice trailed away, but he never took his eyes off Dixie. She stuck out her tongue playfully, clasped his left paw and closed her eyes again. He knew that tomorrow there would be a shiny pair of scissors, a fresh razor, and clean towels waiting for him next to the basin in the bathroom. He lay down to smoke the day's last cigarette and carefully blew out the candle that flickered on the ornate bedside table. Soon Bones began to snore.

He mused that they had definitely climbed to the mountaintop and seen the other side. They had emerged from the fog and embers—crawling from the wreckage, as it were—and there appeared to be no physical scars. The psychological ones might appear later, but he was confident in the fact that he had become one with his soul. There were other places and other sacraments to explore, but for now he was at peace. And after all, it was spring in Austin. What a long, strange trip, indeed.

CHAPTER
TWENTY-FIVE

Lefty was awakened in the rocker on the high front porch by a feminine hand on his cheek. It was warm and soft and smelled of lavender. For the moment, he kept his eyes closed and enjoyed her touch. He thought of where he had been and where he might go. His comfortable womb was interrupted by the sound of the counterbalanced weights inside the workings of an old window frame in the house next door. Like nails on a chalkboard, it screeched until the window was completely open and the top half of an extremely good-looking and buxom Asian woman appeared.

"Hey, Mistah Lefty! You get up now! You don't want miss own party, do you? I'll be light down."

It was Lee, Cal's wife, who had disturbed his serene nap and was now yammering on about *his* party and how she would be "light down." What the hell was this all about? Trying to disengage himself from the minutiae of these little niceties, he slowly began to rock, with his eyes still closed and the fragrant hand on his face.

Soon, a familiar voice called to him from above, "Honey, could you come up here and help me get the card tables out of the attic? I don't want to fall and ruin the party."

Lefty thought, *Good heavens! That's Dixie's voice calling from upstairs. So who in the hell has their hand on my face?* Lefty's brain shot into overdrive and he bolted upright. There, standing over him, was Connie. And behind her, seated in the rocker facing him, was a very familiar face, indeed. With a wicked grin, Pancho was patiently waiting for his friend to come to his senses and join the party. Ever since Connie and Pancho had married a while back, with Lefty and Dixie being the only attendants at the ceremony, they had become an inseparable quartet after finally "getting off the bus." They had moved to Austin and built a grand house on Leathal Lane in the close-knit neighborhood just around the corner from Lefty and Dixie, where they found themselves to be very, very happy.

Soon, Pancho sat up in his seat and asked Lefty, "You kind of liked my wife's hand fondling your face, didn't you? Ah, yes, yes...I saw that." His eyes had dropped to glance at Lefty's protrusion. "I always knew you 'dressed' to the left, old pal. As always, it 'fits' you."

Lefty blushed and looked to see if there were adjustments to be made, and finding none of immediate need, he rose and embraced his old friend warmly. After all the formalities were over, the three joined in a five-armed bear hug and made their way inside.

"Oh, shit, I forgot about Dixie. Honey, I'm on my way up."

Dixie called down to him in response, "Don't worry about it, you imbecile. I got them down already. Is everyone else here?"

This threw Lefty for another loop, and he turned to see Pancho and Connie look away as if they were in on a joke that he wasn't. With confusion in his voice, Lefty slowly asked, "Who is 'everyone else'? And why am I the only one who doesn't know?"

"That's because it was supposed to be a surprise, you schmo," Pancho admitted. "Well, the cat is out of the barn again. Jilly and that husband of hers are making the drive from Florida as we speak. They haven't left 'the rock'—as they call the Keys, you know—since she started popping out little Jillys. They were just a little delayed, wouldn't you know it. They're in high spirits, though, and it shouldn't be long now before they arrive. Why don't we see if we can drum up a cocktail? What do you say?"

Lefty watched the woman of his dreams glide down the staircase to stand at his side. He tried to come up with some lame excuse not to start another bacchanal, but was able to come up with only, "Jeez, Pancho, it might be a little early for that. Do you think we really ought to?"

Pancho bellowed, "I guarantee you that somewhere in this fine, fine world of ours, there is some bull-goose loony tending bar and buying rounds for the house. I just think that it would be a crime *not* to accommodate his wishes and to be gentlemanly about it!" Pancho prodded the girls down the long hallway in the direction of the kitchen like a general leading his forces.

Dixie called out, "Who wants a beverage?"

In unison, Lefty and Pancho said, "If you're waiting on us, you got your hat on backward."

Pancho lingered behind with his friend for a moment before saying, "I thought I might deliver this one personally. It would save on the postage." He handed Lefty an envelope before scooting down the hall to catch up with the girls.

Lefty recognized the familiar block lettering on the front of the envelope and quietly opened it. Already knowing what it would say, Lefty smiled as he read: "Where to?"